TERRI REED

At an early age Terri Reed discovered the wonderful world of fiction and declared she would one day write a book. Now she is fulfilling that dream and enjoys writing for Steeple Hill Books. Her second book, *A Sheltering Love,* was a 2006 RITA® Award finalist and a 2005 National Readers' Choice Award finalist. Her book *Strictly Confidential,* book five of the Faith at the Crossroads continuity series, took third place in the 2007 American Christian Fiction Writers Book of the Year Award, and *Her Christmas Protector* took third place in 2008. She is an active member of both Romance Writers of America and American Christian Fiction Writers. She resides in the Pacific Northwest with her college-sweetheart husband, two wonderful children and an array of critters. When not writing, she enjoys spending time with her family and friends, gardening and playing with her dogs.

You can write to Terri at P.O. Box 19555 Portland, OR 97280. Visit her on the web at www.loveinspiredauthors.com, leave comments on her blog at www.ladiesofsuspense.blogspot.com or email her at terrireed@sterling.net.

STEPHANIE NEWTON

penned her first suspense story—complete with illustrations—at the age of twelve, but didn't write seriously until her youngest child was in first grade. She lives in northwest Florida, where she gains inspiration from the sugar-white sand, the blue-green water of the Gulf of Mexico and the many unusual and interesting things you see when you live on the beach. You can find her most often enjoying the water with her family, or at their church, where her husband is the pastor. Visit Stephanie at her website, www.stephanienewton.net, or send an email to newtonwriter@gmail.com.

HOLIDAY HAVOC

Terri Reed
Stephanie Newton

Steeple
Hill®

Published by Steeple Hill Books™

STEEPLE HILL BOOKS

Steeple
Hill®

Recycling programs
for this product may
not exist in your area.

ISBN-13: 978-0-373-67438-1

HOLIDAY HAVOC

Copyright © 2010 by Harlequin Books S.A.

The publisher acknowledges the copyright holders of the individual works as follows:

YULETIDE SANCTUARY
Copyright © 2010 by Terri Reed

CHRISTMAS TARGET
Copyright © 2010 by Stephanie Newton

www.SteepleHill.com

Printed in U.S.A.

CONTENTS

YULETIDE SANCTUARY
Terri Reed

To Teal and Kim, for being my sisters and loving my children so well.

I will give you a new heart and put a new spirit within you; I will take the heart of stone out of your flesh and give you a heart of flesh.

—*Ezekiel* 36:26

ONE

From the top of a sandy berm skirting the beach, the man barely noticed the bitter cold or the churning surf of the Pacific Ocean off the coast of Oregon. His focus remained on his target.

A feral smile curved his scarred mouth. He couldn't have planned their reunion better. Seemed fate was on his side. Finally. His prey, who'd ruined his life, was alone and vulnerable. Just how he liked his women.

She was just up ahead, walking down the deserted beach with a sketch pad tucked under her arm. Her dark hair whipped about her head in the chilling December wind.

Time was of the essence. It would only be a matter of hours before his ruse was discovered.

His pulse sped up as he shuffled through the tall scrub grass, keeping his gaze fixed on her. On Lauren.

The burning need to avenge his pain seethed

white-hot in his veins. *Patience,* he cautioned himself. He had to capture her quickly and carefully in case some nosy busybody looking out the window of their insulated, Christmas-festooned little home decided to interfere.

He stuck his hand inside the pocket of his long, black leather coat and fingered the syringe of ketamine he'd stolen from a veterinarian clinic outside Burbank. He'd intended to use it on Lauren's mother. Unfortunately, the old bat hadn't been home when he'd broken in. But he'd learned where to find Lauren just the same while tossing the place. He'd then stolen a motorcycle and had ridden straight through from L.A. to this sleepy little Oregon town.

And now Lauren was only a hundred yards away from him, totally unaware that her life was about to end in a drawn-out masterpiece of torture. The familiar thrill of the kill rushed through his body. His breath quickened and the sound of it mingled with the roar of the surf.

Rushing water greedily devoured the beach. The rising tide ebbed and flowed, closer and closer to where she walked. Like him. Closer and closer.

A hulking rock loomed ahead with barnacle crusted tide pools at its base visible in the waning evening light. The waves swelled as the wind picked up. The salty air dampened his clothes and filled his nostrils. The man reached the flat sand of the beach, his scarred legs protesting the excursion. He ignored the pain as he pushed himself to move faster.

Soon, very soon, the plans he'd meticulously plotted over the past five years would come to fruition. Revenge would taste sweet.

As sweet as Lauren's tears.

A woman's sharp, desperate cry broke through Sean Matthews's jogger's trance.

His heart lurched and beach sand sprayed, stinging his shins as his long stride shortened abruptly. Mind racing through possible emergencies, he swung his attention toward the bluff above him.

In the twilight of dusk, it was difficult to spot anything beyond the interior lights that randomly dotted the windows and the strings of colored Christmas lights decorating the eaves of the resorts and cottages of the small town of Cannon Beach. High berms covered with tall grass provided a barrier between the buildings and the ocean. He didn't see anyone.

His gaze scanned the coastline, taking in Haystack Rock, a 235-foot monolith jutting out of the surf. The rising tide stirred the cold swells into white, foam-capped waves that rushed up toward the dryer sand and then quickly retreated, leaving wet, dark patterns in their wake. Mist blowing in on the evening breeze dampened Sean's hair and cooled his sweat until a chill chased down his spine.

Overhead, a gull's caw echoed the scream he'd heard.

He frowned. He hadn't imagined the cry, had he?

He scanned the area once again.

Wait!

His gaze snagged on two figures up ahead. A woman ran through the tide pools toward Sean. A man, dressed in a long black coat with a black beanie covering his head and a scarf wrapped around most of his face, was chasing her. The woman slipped, landing hard on rocks. She cried out.

As the man lunged for the woman, something glinted in his hand. She swung her arms, trying to fend him off. She lifted her head, her gaze seeming to bore right into Sean.

"Help! Help me!" she cried.

Sean's gut clenched. This was no couple romping through wavelets. The woman was in trouble. Reflexively, he reached inside his sweatshirt pocket for his cell phone but came up empty. Frustration spiraled through him. He'd left the thing in his truck parked at the edge of the public access road.

Knowing he was the only help available, Sean sprang into action, his feet thwacking against the sand as he ran toward the man. "Hey, hey! Leave her alone."

The man paused and swung his head toward Sean. Though Sean couldn't make out the attacker's features, there was no mistaking the malice in his dark eyes before he scrambled away and ran in the opposite direction, moving with an odd but fast gait toward the sandbank. He quickly disappeared into the tall grass.

Sean navigated a slippery, algae-covered tide pool to where the woman, seated in a puddle, was violently struggling to yank her pinned ankle from a rock crevice. She was petite with delicate features and brunette hair falling past her shoulders. She visibly shivered in her wet pink sport jacket and sweatpants.

Lord, show me how to help this woman.

Sean knelt down next to her and met her gaze. Her toffee-colored eyes brimmed with panic and wariness. "It's going to be okay," he said. "Do you have a cell phone with you?"

"I do." She reached into her jacket pocket and

came up empty. "It must have fallen out." Panic echoed in her words as she continued to wrestle with her trapped foot.

Calling 911 would have to wait until they reached his truck.

"Let me try to get your foot out."

"Did you see him?" She stopped struggling and braced her hands against the mussel-encrusted lava rock.

Sean searched her face. "That man who attacked you? Yes."

She lifted a hand to her forehead. "I didn't imagine him."

Okay, that was weird. "He was real. Do you know him?"

She shook her head, her dark bangs sticking to her high forehead. Even wet and bedraggled, she was pretty in a natural, girl-next-door way. "No. I mean, yes. No. It just couldn't be." She glanced over her shoulder. "Please, tell me he's gone. Of course he's gone. He's in prison. No way could he have gotten out." She started to rock slightly.

She wasn't making sense; maybe the trauma of being attacked had been too much for her. The need to take care of her rose sharply in Sean. He fought the inclination. He'd come to this small community so he wouldn't have to take responsibility for anyone ever again, but he couldn't fight who he was any more than he could have let that man attack her without stepping in.

Sean had to set her free and get her help. Turning his focus to her foot, he noticed that her ankle was trapped between a deep red starfish, jagged black rock and white barnacles. Using his fingers for leverage, he pried at one of the prickly limbs of the starfish, his nose filling with the pungent scent of decay and brine as he pulled. The sharp, pointy bumps of the outer body bit into his cold fingers as he tugged and twisted, but the creature wouldn't budge.

Frustration and disappointment chomped through him. He contemplated his next move. Water crashed over the bed of lava rock, filling the various pools as the tide rolled in. Soon the whole area would be completely under water. He wrested a mussel shell free from the rock and sharpened its edge against the coarse stone.

The chatter of the woman's teeth echoed in his ears. He paused before pulling off the sweatshirt covering his running T-shirt. "Take off your wet jacket and put this on."

Her pale hand, the fingertips smudged black, clutched at the neck of her fleece jacket. "I can't."

"I'll help you." He leaned toward her and reached for the zipper.

She drew back with a squawk.

He held up his hands. "Look, I'm not going to hurt you. I promise. Do you have something on under your jacket?"

"A tank top. But that doesn't mean I'm going to take off my jacket." Her brown eyes flashed with warning.

Sean sighed, a mixture of empathy and irritation running hot in his veins. Modesty shouldn't be a priority at a time like this. "You're soaked and freezing. A prime candidate for hypothermia. Here." He pushed his sweatshirt into her hands. "Put this on while I try to get this starfish to let go."

He turned away from her and quickly forced the sharpened edge of the shell beneath one of the rays. He needed to hurry. The sun had begun its descent beneath the horizon. Soon it would be dark and he'd be working blind.

Next to him, he could hear her struggling. The frustrated exhales. The sharp gasps of air.

"You okay?" he asked.

She huffed. "No. I guess I'll need your help." Resignation echoed in her words. "The zipper's… well, stuck."

He turned toward her again, fiddling with the zipper until it gave way. Her right hand braced against the rock, she lifted her left arm so Sean could yank off the jacket. As he moved to pull the rest of the light coat away, she grabbed his sweatshirt from her lap and held it against the bright yellow tank top.

Why was she so modest, especially in the midst of an emergency?

Sean quickly pulled the wet jacket from her right arm.

Then he knew.

Red, puckered flesh marred the skin running from her forearm to the top of her shoulder and disappeared into her sleeveless shirt. He sucked in a quick breath.

Please, Father, not again.

Lauren Curtis dropped her gaze to the dark, porous lava rock.

She couldn't stand to see the pity and revulsion her scars always generated. And this big, thoughtful man was no different from everyone else. Precisely why no one, save her doctors, was allowed to see her ugliness.

Oh, Lord, why did this have to happen?

As she had a thousand times before, she sent the question upward. But for the first time in five years, she wasn't referring to the horrible nightmare that had derailed her life and killed her dreams. Now she referred to this moment in time.

When her nightmare had reappeared.

She bit her lip. But it just couldn't be.

Once again she glanced over her shoulder, unsurprised that no one was there. The man who had attacked her wasn't Adrian. Adrian was locked up for the rest of his life. She'd been reassured of that over and over again, every time she called the police in a panic, when she'd thought she was being followed or that someone had broken into her home. She'd called so many times in the last five years that it was embarrassing, but their reply never changed. Adrian was in jail. She was safe. So why didn't she *feel* safe?

She trembled and quickly pulled her rescuer's sweatshirt over her head, then tugged it down to her waist, out of the water's reach. His scent wafted from the well-worn material. Spicy and very, very masculine. She snuggled into the too-large sweatshirt, the fleece inside soft and warm against her cold skin, and prayed he could help her.

"Thank you for giving up your sweatshirt," she whispered, glancing up. She met his clear blue gaze, so like a summer sky. He regarded her with cautious kindness.

"No problem. I'm Sean Matthews."

She liked his name almost as much as she liked his deep baritone voice. "I'm Lauren. Lauren Curtis."

"Hi, Lauren." He held her gaze for a moment before turning his attention back to her predicament.

In the waning light, she watched his arms bunch and flex as his large, capable hands worked at freeing her ankle. She couldn't even feel pain, her flesh was so numb from the frigid water.

"What were you doing out here?" he asked.

"I wanted to sketch the sunset. Then Ad—" She couldn't bring herself to say his name. "That man came charging down the beach at me."

"I saw something in his hand. What was it?"

Lauren thought for a moment. "I'm not sure. I didn't get a good look. I think it may have been a knife."

Sean's jaw tightened. "Do you live around here?"

"Yes. My house is just up the way."

"That guy may have seen you walking alone and followed you," Sean said. "We'll need to report the attack as soon as possible."

Did her assailant know where she lived? Fresh

fear congealed in her limbs, turning her blood to ice.

The starfish shifted. Involuntarily, she cried out as her ankle throbbed. To keep her mind from the pain and fear, she asked, "Do you live around here?"

He nodded. "Recently moved."

So he wasn't a longtime local or tourist. A transplant, like herself. "Where are you from?"

He hesitated. His lips pressed together for a moment. "Portland."

"It was a blessing that you were out jogging," Lauren stated.

Was he the type who believed in fate, or did he believe, as she did, that God was the only one in control? Either way, he gave no reply.

The pressure on her ankle eased up the second time the starfish moved.

Sean sat back on his haunches. "Better?"

"Much."

"Can you move your foot at all?"

Pushing her hands against the rocks, she tried to pull herself free. She let out a guttural groan of pain. Her foot remained wedged in the crevice. "I...I can't." She was tired and cold, and frustration beat a steady rhythm at her temple.

Sean nodded. "Relax. I'll keep trying." He continued to pry at the starfish.

Chilled to the core, Lauren realized parts of her were numb. What she wouldn't do for a nice warm shower and her big down comforter.

"Lauren!"

Startled, she blinked and realized she'd rested back onto the rock. Propping herself up on her elbows, she said, "I'm sorry. I'm getting your sweatshirt dirty."

The corner of Sean's mouth lifted in a half smile. "Forget the shirt. Just concentrate on staying upright. I know you're probably in shock, but I really need you to stay focused here."

Lauren studied him as he worked to release her ankle. He was exceptionally handsome with his windblown, thick, dark auburn hair shorn close to his ears, and his strong jaw shadowed by a late-day beard.

Snap out of it, Lauren. He wasn't Prince Charming and she wasn't a damsel in distress. She stifled a scoff. Okay, maybe she was in distress—or more likely hypothermia—but this was no fairy tale. She'd stopped believing in fairy tales a long time ago.

Her eyes met Sean's raised brow. "It's getting dark," she said inanely.

The sun had disappeared over the horizon and dusk was rapidly turning into night. The roar of the waves echoed across the shore. Normally, Lauren loved the beach at night. She'd found that was the time when she felt most connected to God. Being attacked and then trapped in a tide pool had put a damper on things, however.

"Lauren?"

"Yes?"

Sean moved behind her. "I need you to relax. I'm going to try pulling you out."

Lauren breathed in deep and tried to quell the tremors running through her body, but the cold stiffening her limbs thwarted her efforts. Sean's hand slid beneath her shoulders without hesitation and fitted her against his chest. She didn't have time to react to his warmth before he tugged her backward hard. Pain shot up her leg. She gritted her teeth to keep from screaming.

Then, to her amazement and relief, her foot popped loose from its rocky prison, minus her tennis shoe.

"I'm free. Oh, thank you," she cried. "Thank you so much."

He helped her to a full sitting position, then knelt beside her feet. Her right foot had swollen like a balloon. With a light touch he ran his hands over her foot, ankle and up her calf. "I can't tell if it's broken. Thankfully, your pant leg protected the skin. We'd better get you to the hospital."

She recoiled at the idea and her stomach turned. "Do I have to go?"

"Yes, you have to." Sean unexpectedly scooped her up in his arms, making her heart jump. "Now, just relax."

"I really, really hate hospitals," she said, wishing she could make him understand just how much she loathed the sights, the sounds and especially the antiseptic smells. "I'd rather wait and go to my doctor's office tomorrow."

Sean shook his head. "You need to be looked at tonight."

She thought up an excuse. "But the hospital is so far away."

He arched an eyebrow. "Seaside is only ten miles. We'll call the police from my truck on the way."

"I really don't want to go." Hospitals equaled pain, torturous and agonizing pain. From the moment she'd awakened in one after the Nightmare to the day she'd been released, all she'd known was pain. Her follow-up appointments were always at her doctor's office, never at the hospital. The thought of returning to one, even for a minor injury, made her heart race. On some level she knew she was being irrational. She needed to have her ankle looked at. But still... She shuddered.

One side of his mouth quirked. "I'll stay with you."

She could either make a big stink or accept his kindness. Right now, she was too worn out to argue. The one thing she knew was that she didn't want to be alone. But could she trust him? "Promise?"

"Promise."

As he carried her across the sand, she couldn't resist snuggling into the cocoon of his arms. For this moment, she needed to trust him. She really didn't have any other option. She was at this man's mercy. Praying she wasn't making a mistake, she laid her cheek against his broad chest. The rapid cadence of his heartbeat lulled her senses. He'd stay with her. He'd promised. She closed her eyes, allowing herself this one moment of comfort.

Because she knew the pain of how easily promises were broken.

The harsh, white overhead lights of the exam room brought back bad memories of month upon excruciating month Lauren had spent in Torrance Memorial Burn Center. Grafting, physical therapy and unending pain. Fear nagged at the edges of her mind, threatening to bring back the Nightmare. She closed her eyes and forced herself to stay in the moment.

She sat on the exam table with her throbbing leg propped up, waiting for the doctor to arrive. Ten minutes ago, the nurse had chased Sean out so she could help Lauren change out of her soaked sweatpants and into a gown. Now a thin blanket lay draped over her bare legs and, though dry, the light material did little to keep her warm. A chill prickled her skin, but she knew it was only partially triggered by the room's temperature.

Sean had called 911 on the way to the hospital. The police would be here any minute to take her statement. What would she tell them? They'd think she was crazy if she suggested the possibility that Adrian was here in Cannon Beach. She knew that couldn't be true. Surely Detective Jarvis would have warned her if Adrian had been released from prison.

A squeaking noise echoed in the room seconds before the curtain was yanked aside. An orderly wearing blue scrubs pushed a wheelchair with a wobbly wheel into the room. He was slender with bushy hair and a thick beard that covered his lips. His smile revealed chipped teeth.

"Doc Allen says you're to come down to radiology," he said in a gravelly voice.

Not comfortable with the guy and wanting to see her own physician, who was on call, she asked, "Where's Dr. Sorensen?"

"He'll be along." The orderly gestured. "Let's get you into the chair."

He reached for her. She automatically shrank back, but he was quicker. His meaty, latex-encased hand closed over her arm in a firm grip as he steadied her while she maneuvered into the wheelchair, keeping her weight off her injured leg. When he released her, she rubbed her arm where she was sure she'd have marks from his fingers. "I want to see the nurse."

"She's busy." He wheeled her out of the exam room, past the empty nurses' station, festively decorated with garlands and little stockings strung across a short desk wall bearing the names of the staff members.

Forcing back her anxiety, Lauren hung on tight to the chair arms. The orderly wheeled her down a dimly lit corridor and then through swinging doors into a room with an X-ray machine and a table.

"Where's the technician?" she asked, surveying the empty room as unease coiled low in her belly. She didn't see anyone in the technician's booth.

There was another closed door at the other end of the room with a name plate for the radiologist. No light seeped from beneath the crack under the door. Where was everyone?

The orderly's bushy eyebrows drew together. "He should be here." With a sigh, he pushed the chair toward the middle of the room and locked the wheels. "I'll go see if I can round him up," he said and strode out, leaving Lauren alone.

Agitation slithered across the nape of her neck. A whisper of noise from behind her jump-started her pulse. Twisting at the waist, she tried to see who'd entered. "Hello?"

No one answered. The lights blinked out, throwing the room into pitch-darkness.

What was going on?

Her mouth went dry with fear.

Terrified and feeling trapped, Lauren tried to get up, but her ankle wouldn't bear weight and the footrest on the wheelchair kept her from simply bailing out of the chair and crawling to the door.

Determined to escape, she bent over the side of the chair and fumbled with the wheel locks. The musky scent of a man's cologne filled her head, making her world spin with horror. She knew that smell. Her heart slammed against her ribs. But it couldn't be!

Panic built in her chest as she gripped the wheels and struggled to turn the chair. Someone had hold of the handles! The chair jerked backward.

A scream tore from her.

TWO

The sound of feet pounding on linoleum echoed in the room as Lauren's scream died away in the dark. The door crashed open and the overhead lights came back on. Dr. Sorensen, Sean and two uniformed police officers rushed inside. Relief infused her, making her more conscious of the ache in her ankle.

"What's wrong?" Sean asked as he knelt beside the wheelchair, concern etched on his face.

Shaking with fear, she gripped his hand, thankful for his presence. "After the orderly left, someone else came in."

Adrian was here. Terror knotted her stomach, but she couldn't bring herself to say the words. How many times before had she thought the same thing, only to be told he hadn't been there? The therapist she saw had said she suffered from post-traumatic stress disorder and her paranoia was a symptom. And this was what was happening now.

She was being paranoid, imagining things. She had to be.

"No one came out," one of the officers commented.

The older of the two officers, a man with graying hair and a definite paunch, went to the technician's booth and peered inside. "No one here."

He walked to the other end of the room and tried to open the door to the radiologist's office. "It's locked."

Lauren gripped Sean's hands tighter as she fought to control her dread. "I tried to wheel myself out but someone had hold of the handles. I could feel him behind me." *I could smell him.*

Stark memories of her attacker shuddered through her, making her shake violently.

No, no. Adrian couldn't be here. He was locked up for good in Southern California. Her imagination was just running wild again.

"You couldn't move the chair because the wheels are locked," Dr. Sorensen said.

"No. I'd unlocked them." Hadn't she?

She saw the glance the two officers exchanged. They thought she was nuts. Maybe she was. The police in L.A. had certainly come to the conclusion she was.

"I need to make a phone call," she said. Calling

Detective Jarvis was the only way to put her mind at ease. He'd been nothing but patient with her all the other times she'd panicked, thinking Adrian was around every corner, in each dark shadow.

"Okay, okay. Let's get this done first," Sean said in a placating voice.

Clearly he was humoring her, and she didn't blame him. She knew she sounded like she was off her rocker. But someone *had* been here. She was sure of it.

Sean glanced up at the officers. "Can you wait to take her statement until after the X-rays?"

"Sure," the older officer said. "We'll wait outside."

Standing, Sean said, "Doctor, can we hurry this along?"

"Of course." Dr. Sorensen pushed the chair forward. "We'll be as quick as possible."

They weren't quick enough, as far as Lauren was concerned. And all the movement only aggravated her injury. She wanted to get away from here, away from this horrible place and back to her cottage where she could call Detective Jarvis and finally feel safe again.

When the X-ray was complete, the officers took her statement about the attack on the beach.

"You didn't get a good look at his face?" Officer

Devon asked. He was a beefy man with a ruddy complexion and kind eyes.

"No. He wore a hat and a scarf so only his eyes were visible. He had dark eyes." Just like Adrian. She had to contact Detective Jarvis. Should she ask them to call the LAPD? "Could you…?"

The older officer's dark eyebrows rose. "Yes?"

Deciding she couldn't handle appearing foolish in front of Sean, she resolved to make the call in private once she arrived home. That way she wouldn't have to explain the details or find out in a public venue that she was truly letting paranoia get the better of her, again. "Could you follow us to my house?" she improvised.

The two officers exchanged a glance before nodding. Officer Devon asked, "Do you have someone who can stay with you? Or somewhere else you can stay for a few days while we search for this guy?"

Lauren bit her lip. Her mother was in Los Angeles and Lauren didn't have any friends here. She shook her head.

"We'll see about getting you some protection then," the older man, Officer Kay, said before they retreated.

That made her feel infinitely better. Maybe she wouldn't have to call Detective Jarvis after all. He'd just tell her the same thing he always had. This way, she could have people around to make her feel safe without having to disturb him again.

Sean wheeled her back to the exam room. His presence gave her a measure of peace. Fortunately, the X-ray showed her ankle wasn't broken. She'd suffered only a bad sprain and some nasty bruises. She took some pain medication as the doctor wrapped a hard, molded plastic splint and a bandage around her ankle and part of her calf. A nurse came in and helped her into blue surgical pants so she could leave the hospital. In her lap, she held a bag containing her wet sweatpants.

"So, I can count on you, Mr. Matthews?" Dr. Sorensen talked over Lauren's head to Sean as the two men rejoined her in the exam room.

"Yes, of course."

Lauren had heard the slight hint of reservation in Sean's voice. She shifted uncomfortably in the wheelchair to peer up at him while keeping her bound leg propped up. A gymnast she wasn't. "Count on him for what?" she asked.

She didn't like that they'd apparently discussed her outside the exam room.

Dr. Sorensen flashed a patient smile. "Mr. Matthews has agreed to help you out for the next few days while you stay off that ankle."

A rock dropped in the pit of her stomach and her gaze flew to Sean's guarded expression. He'd kept his promise to stay with her at the hospital, but he obviously wasn't happy to be asked to tend to her further. A reluctant Good Samaritan for sure.

How could she blame him? Why would he want to help a stranger? Especially someone as hideous as her. Sure, covered up she looked normal. But Sean had already glimpsed some of the horrible scars that made her look and feel ugly. He'd be repulsed if he saw the rest. Just like Greg had been. Her former fiancé had taken one look and turned green. He'd tried to hide his repulsion at first. Tried to stay positive, but when the doctors had finally declared she was as healed as she would be, Greg had bailed. All of his promises turned to dust in the wake of his exit out of her life.

Even her friends' visits had dwindled to the point where she knew the relationships hadn't been deep. Not deep enough to withstand her ugliness.

And Sean probably thought she was a little nuts as well, after the way she'd acted in the X-ray room.

Besides, depending on him would only set her

up for more heartache. She couldn't depend on anyone.

"I don't even know him," she told the doctor. "Besides, the police officer said they'd provide protection."

"I know Sean's family. They're good people. And the officers will still do their part," Dr. Sorensen said in a firm tone, "but you're going to need some care, since you're not going to be very ambulatory for at least a few days."

Familiar protective barriers went up all around her heart and her mind. Her gaze shifted to Sean. "I don't need your pity any more than I need your help."

Sean arched an eyebrow. "How does my helping you constitute pity?"

She frowned, struggling for a logical answer and just as quickly gave up finding one. "It just does."

Amusement entered Sean's clear blue eyes. "Are you always so stubborn?"

"Are you always so annoying?" she countered, even as she realized how awful she sounded. She was tired, freaked out and ready to just be alone in her own space with the doors tightly locked and a police car outside.

He grinned. Lauren's breath caught in her throat.

He definitely belonged in a fairy tale, not her night-mare. What was he doing dashing into her dark corner?

Dr. Sorensen's chuckle reminded her to let out the air she'd trapped in her chest.

"I'll let you two work this out. Lauren, I expect to see you back here in a few days."

"I'll make sure she comes," Sean said.

Surprised by the determination in Sean's voice, Lauren stared.

Dr. Sorensen excused himself and walked out.

Lauren forced herself to focus. This was her ordeal and she'd go it alone, just as she had all along. "I don't need your help."

"You have a friend we can call?"

She pressed her lips together, hating to admit that she'd kept to herself since coming to Oregon. It was better that way. Safer. The silence stretched and she knew she had to give some sort of answer. "I don't know very many people here."

"Family?"

"Mom lives in Los Angeles. Dad's dead. No siblings."

A flash of sympathy clouded his eyes. "Will your mother come?"

Yes, which was another problem. Lauren didn't

want to have her mother hovering over her. Again. "I'm sure she will."

"Then you're stuck with me until your mother arrives. Besides, you've had a traumatic experience tonight—you shouldn't be alone right now."

Lauren's ankle throbbed and her head ached. The fight drained out of her. He was right. She had had another harrowing experience, even if it had ended well. This time around. "Okay, fine. You can help me. For now."

He grasped the handles of the wheelchair and began to push her toward the exit. The cheery Christmas decorations did little to elevate Lauren's mood. A shiver of residual fear traipsed over her skin. The strange sensation of being watched slithered along her nerves. She glanced around.

The waiting area was jam-packed with patients, seemingly uninterested in her, while nurses and orderlies bustled about doing their jobs. Everything seemed normal. A passing doctor with a stethoscope hanging around his neck smiled when he caught her eye.

She dropped her gaze to her folded hands. Maybe she was going a little crazy. Maybe she'd imagined the whole episode in the X-ray room. Just like she'd imagined Adrian in the parking lot of the supermarket three years ago, or imagined she'd seen him lurking in the shadows at the library last year. She saw Adrian's face every time she glanced out a darkened window; every time she entered a room she braced herself for his attack. Her therapist said it would take time for her to stop reliving the Nightmare. She'd hoped moving far away from every reminder would be enough. Apparently not.

She peeked up at Sean. Good of him to be so nice about the whole thing, even if he didn't realize what he was letting himself in for by promising to take care of her.

And though he'd been true to his word thus far, Lauren couldn't allow her lonely heart to become attached to him. To anyone.

She couldn't survive being rejected again.

On the drive back to Cannon Beach, Sean thought about Lauren's claim that someone had been in radiology with her. First the attack on the beach, then this?

He could understand her paranoia, especially in light of the trauma that Dr. Sorensen had hinted at and that Sean had seen evidence of on her arm. His curiosity was piqued, but he shied away from asking. He was already more involved than he should be. The less he knew the better. Much less emotionally taxing that way. For them both.

But just as he'd been unable to ignore her cries for help on the beach, he found he couldn't stop himself from wanting to help her now. From her insistence that she could go it alone, he had a feeling she didn't want him caring for her any more than he wanted to. She'd sounded a lot like some of the teens he'd dealt with over the years. Wanting so badly to be independent and self-sufficient, they refused to acknowledge the need for others.

The need for God.

He wondered about Lauren's relationship with God. He'd noted she'd called his timing on the beach a blessing. Was her use of the word an indication of her faith or was it just a fitting term that held no significance to her? And if she didn't have faith, would she be open to hearing about God's love for her and His promises for her life?

Sean's stomach dropped. Didn't matter. He wasn't going down that path. Sean could keep an eye on her until her mother arrived, but he couldn't help her. He couldn't help anyone.

He forced himself to concentrate as Lauren directed him to her cottage. The headlights of the police cruiser reflected in his rearview mirror.

"Sean?"

"Hmm?

"I don't really know you."

He tilted his head. "No, you don't."

"Why should I trust you?" Lauren asked, radiating vulnerability in the set of her jaw, the guarded expression in her lovely eyes. "I mean, you could be an ax murderer or a…psychopath, for all I know."

"I'm not an ax murderer." He allowed a half smile. "Or a psychopath. I promise."

"Then who are you?"

His gut tightened. Dr. Sorensen had asked the same question and had seemed satisfied that Sean was Mary Shannon's nephew. Lauren didn't know Aunt Mary, so that response wouldn't work for her. She was asking him a question she had every right to ask, but he didn't know how to answer without looking back at his mistakes. He settled on the present truth. The past was best left buried. "I'm renovating a historic bed-and-breakfast on Maple Street."

"Shannon's?"

He nodded, not surprised she knew the place. "My aunt Mary owns it."

Mary had given him a purpose when she'd invited him to come to Cannon Beach, never once asking why he'd needed to leave Portland. She undoubtedly knew some of the facts, but not all. No one would know the whole truth, save God.

"Okay, that tells me what you do, but not if I should trust you."

Sean considered her for a moment. The warm moonlight reflected in her amber-colored eyes was so honest and full of curiosity. Her dark hair had clumped together in places as it had dried, reminding him how close to danger she'd been. Returning his gaze to the road, he said, "Search your heart, Lauren. You'll find the answer."

In return, she regarded him thoughtfully for a heartbeat. "Do you believe in God?"

"Yes." His answer came readily. He'd never lost his belief in his Savior. Only in himself.

Her full lips curved into a pleased smile. "Which church do you attend?"

His heart rebelled at the question. He wasn't prepared to explain why he hadn't stepped inside a church in six months.

He was saved from answering when he pulled in front of her cottage and parked on the sandy shoulder of the short street that led to the beach. Small clapboard houses with even smaller yards lined both sides. A typical beach access street.

The officers parked behind him, jumped out of their vehicle and hurried toward the house, their heavy-duty flashlights glowing bright. Several minutes later, they came back to the street.

Officer Kay leaned inside Sean's driver's side window. "We walked the perimeter. All the windows are secure and the doors locked tight. Do you want us to search inside?"

Sean turned to Lauren. Her eyes looked so big in the moonlight. "What do you think?"

"You're sure the back windows haven't been tampered with?"

"Not that we could see. There are no scratches, the screens are intact and the windows are closed."

"I'd appreciate if you went inside," she said.

"Key?" Officer Kay held out his hand.

Lauren dug into the bag that held her sweatpants and produced a single key on a silver square key chain. She handed it over to the officer.

A few moments later, lights glowed inside the cottage as the officers searched the rooms.

Officer Devon jogged back to the cab of Sean's truck. "It's safe to go in."

Lauren leaned toward the window. "How can you be sure that guy from the beach won't come after you've left?"

"We'll sit tight out here for a while and then have a patrol car drive through the neighborhood," the officer replied. "I don't think you have to worry about your attacker coming back. Most likely he saw you walking alone and took advantage of the situation. A purely random event. We'll find him."

Sensing how upset Lauren was, Sean reached out a hand and covered hers. After a slight hesitation, she held on tight.

"Thank you, Officer," she said.

"Come on, let's get you inside." Sean carried Lauren from the cab of his truck. Though small sconces by the front door illuminated the porch, all Sean could make out beneath his feet was a stone path and wooden slats. Her lightweight, slim body fit perfectly in the crook of his arms. Her head resting against his chest caused a hot spot over his heart.

He opened the front door and strode inside, shutting the door with the heel of his running shoe.

An overhead light shone from a fancy, antique-looking fixture, flooding the room with soft, yellow warmth. The cottage was small, but cozy. A cold fireplace with a wide wood mantel took up most of a long wall opposite the front door. A short Christmas tree stood unlit in the corner. An overstuffed couch butted up against the front windowpane and an oversize chair sat beside a bookcase lined with volumes.

Very comfortable and homey. A place to come

home to at the end of the day. He might have wanted a house like this for himself once. But not anymore. He didn't deserve comfort.

Two end tables were cluttered with sketch pads and an array of pencils. Apparently, drawing wasn't a casual hobby for her. Maybe he'd check the beach in the morning and see if her sketch pad had survived the tide.

Hardwood floors gleamed around a large, rose-colored area rug. Two arched doorways, one off to the left and the other directly across from the front door, led to darkened rooms.

He took Lauren to the couch and set her down gently, then propped up her injured ankle with a frilly, colorful, flowered throw pillow. She smiled at him gratefully as she sank back with a sigh.

"Can I get you anything? Something to drink or eat?" Sean asked, needing to do something besides stare at her pretty face.

She shook her head and stared at him with wide eyes as if she didn't quite know what to make of him. Did she still question trusting him?

On the table beside her lay an open sketchbook. Thankful for the distraction and a safe topic, he gestured to the book and asked, "May I?"

There was a moment's hesitation before she nodded.

Picking up the pad, he flipped through drawings of the seashore and the quaint town of Cannon Beach. The definition and shading in each picture captured a distinct mood. Details stood out, showing the talent behind the work. The art was in the delicacy of her small, capable hands.

"I like your drawings."

"Thank you."

"Is drawing a hobby or your livelihood?"

Cannon Beach was known for being an artists' colony. She could easily sell her work in any one of the many shops or galleries along the main street.

She looked away but not before he glimpsed pain and regret reflected across her pretty face. "A little of both."

"They're very good. Have you gone to art school?"

"I graduated from the Art Center College of Design in Pasadena, California."

Impressive. "How did you end up in Oregon?"

"I'd been to Cannon Beach as a child and had always remembered how much I adored the community. Then after…" She placed her hand on her shoulder. "I just needed a change."

The scars. How had they happened?

As quick as lightning, compassion infused Sean. His heart twisted with the need to offer comfort.

No, his brain screamed, recoiling from traveling down that road again.

He couldn't reach out and risk failing to help.

"Would you mind dragging over the clothes basket from the hall? The clothes are clean, I just haven't put them away yet. I should change."

Grateful for the change in subject, he set down the sketch pad. "Sure." He brought her the basket, from which she chose a powder-blue sweat suit. "I'll just step out."

Escaping into the kitchen, he found the light switch. The space was small, but had a simple charm. White countertops were scrubbed clean, and the dining area hosted a small, round oak table with four matching chairs. In the center of the table sat a bouquet of flowers. White-and-blue gingham curtains hung at the window above the sink. Morning or evening, the sun would make the place cheery.

Lauren had built herself a nice life. A life he didn't belong in. "What am I doing?" he muttered.

He leaned his forehead against the cool door of the refrigerator. *Lord, I can't do this. I can't help her. I can't help anyone. I've already proven that.*

Grace.

His breath caught. The word reverberated in his head.

He gave a soft, wry laugh. "Yes, Lord, You're big enough to forgive me, but I can't forgive myself." Guilt rode him hard, making him turn away from everyone, even God.

But he couldn't abandon Lauren. She shouldn't have to suffer because he couldn't deal with playing caretaker for a couple of days. He'd help her out. He'd promised.

Just a day or so. Fix her a few meals, see that she was comfortable and safe, until her mother arrived. Not that hard to do. Then he could go back to what he'd come to Cannon Beach for—solitude.

"You can come back in," Lauren called out.

Taking a bracing breath, Sean reentered the living room.

"I should call my mom. Would you mind bringing me the phone?" Lauren asked. "It's on the entryway table."

A light blinked on the phone's square base. "You have a message."

Lauren's eyes widened. Was that panic darkening her gaze?

"Do you want me to play it?"

She nodded.

Sean pushed the button with the play symbol. A woman's voice filled the room. "Hi, dear, it's Mom. Just wanted to remind you I'm leaving on the cruise for the week, but I'll be back in time to come to Cannon Beach for Christmas."

The air left Sean's lungs in a swoosh as he stared at the beautiful stranger he'd rescued and realized there was no getting out of his promise anytime soon.

THREE

"You didn't know your mother was leaving?"

The unmistakable surprise in Sean's voice made Lauren shrug, as she tried not to let on how uncomfortable she was. Having a visitor wasn't something she did often, or ever, really. Other than her mom. "I'd forgotten about the cruise. She told me about it a while ago. I'm not my mother's keeper. She comes and goes as she pleases." At least ever since Lauren had struck out on her own and Mom hadn't been encumbered with taking care of her. "She'll call when she's on her way here."

He considered her, his thoughts veiled. "Then you'll have to come with me back to Aunt Mary's."

Lauren scoffed. "No."

He mimicked her scoff. "Yes."

"I've been enough of a burden to you, I'm not going to trouble your aunt as well," she stated firmly.

"When I called Mary from the hospital to tell her what had happened, she issued the invitation. I didn't bring it up because you said your mom would be coming. But since that's not the case, I know Mary would insist on you staying with us. She's looking forward to meeting you."

Lauren's dander rose. She narrowed her eyes. "You can't just come in and start planning my life."

He held up a hand. "No one's trying to plan or run or control you. This—"

"I disagr—"

"Just hear me out," he interjected, as she had. "It makes more sense for you to stay in the bed-and-breakfast while you're waiting for your mother. I'll be there working and Mary will love the company. She'll never admit as much, but ever since Uncle Bill passed on, she's been lonely. I think you two will hit it off. So, actually, you'll be doing me a favor by distracting my aunt."

Lauren shifted her aching foot on the pillow. Sean sure knew how to turn things around. Lauren wasn't sure she was buying his lonely aunt story. The only lonely people in friendly little Cannon Beach were those who chose to be. Like her.

Worry chomped through her. Staying with him put her at risk. Not physically, but emotionally.

If she stayed with him and his aunt, if she began to care about them and became attached, she'd only be opening herself up for more hurt because eventually she'd leave and go back to her world. She doubted they'd stay in touch. So guarding her heart would have to be paramount.

She had to admit—never to him, though—that she wasn't too keen on staying alone while slightly incapacitated, both physically and now mentally, if the hospital episode tonight was any indication. Whoever that man on the beach had been, he could know where she lived. Even with the police patrolling the area, she didn't feel completely safe.

And the kicker was that if she did agree to stay at the B and B, then there'd really be no need for her mother to even know she'd been injured. Once she heard, she'd insist that either she move here or Lauren return home to L.A. Two equally unacceptable options. And that was all the reason Lauren needed to agree to Sean's offer.

"All right." She nodded. "For your aunt."

He squared his shoulders. "Okay, then. That's settled."

"I'll need to pack a few things."

"Point me in the direction of your suitcase and we'll have you packed in no time."

Waving toward the hall, she gave him instructions. "In my workroom, on the shelf in the closet, there are two small bags."

It was so unlike her to willingly let someone else take control or to let someone so emotionally close. She felt both agitated and relieved. How could that be?

Watching Sean walk from the room, she was struck by his gracefulness. No lumbering or swagger. Just long, purposeful strides. She tried to analyze how she felt about having a man in her house.

On the one hand, it was nice to have someone around. Plus, he seemed generous and caring. She hadn't allowed anyone through the door, literally or metaphorically, in a long time.

Of course, this situation was unique.

But that didn't make letting Sean into her life any easier. She'd ensconced herself in this small town for a reason. The tourists came and went, the locals minded their own business after their initial overtures were rebuffed and she could exist without pity or sympathy because no one was allowed to look beyond the surface.

No one would ever see beneath her scars.

Lauren leaned back on the couch. She had to admit she liked Sean. There was something soothing about him. Something that made her want to rely on him, to relinquish her troubles and worries into his strong, capable hands. And that was why she couldn't allow herself to become dependent on him. Not even for a few days. Because he was just a passing ship in her stormy life. Sooner or later, he'd leave, so the sooner he was gone, the better.

Relaxing, she closed her eyes and let her body sink into the cushions. The pain medication they'd given her at the hospital was finally taking effect. The throbbing in her ankle receded and her head no longer pounded. In the quiet moment, she finally relaxed enough to express her gratitude to God.

Dear Lord, thank You for sending Sean out to the beach this evening. I know You have some purpose for our lives to intersect. Whatever it is, I'm grateful. If only… She bit her lip.

There was no use wishing or praying her life was different, that she would be a whole woman again. A woman who could attract a good-looking, thoughtful man like Sean and be free to see if a relationship developed. Longing hit her with the accuracy of a champion archer.

The medicine must be stirring up such crazy thoughts. She'd resigned herself to never having an intimate relationship because of her scars. She need only to look in the mirror to be reminded that no man would want to touch her hideousness. Greg certainly hadn't, even though, only the month prior to her attack, he'd declared his undying devotion when he'd proposed. His love had been dependent on her outward beauty.

How could she expect anything different from any other man? But she could allow herself a friend, couldn't she? A friend with no strings attached, no expectations. Sean had already seen part of her scar and hadn't recoiled in horror. She'd just have to make sure he never saw the rest. That wouldn't be hard to do, considering her choice of attire.

A small smile touched her heart. Yes, she decided. She could allow Sean to be her friend. Someone to converse with, maybe even laugh with someday. She missed laughing. Sean seemed to be a good-humored man. And kind. And gentle…

Her eyelids drooped.

As long as he didn't try to save her from herself.

She jerked upright as that thought ricocheted around her mind, setting off alarm bells. She'd sent Sean to her workroom.

Oh, no! She gasped softly. She couldn't believe she'd just sent Sean into forbidden territory.

As soon as the door swung open, Sean understood why she referred to this space as her workroom. Several half-finished oil paintings on easels crowded the small area. And more work in progress was stacked against the walls. A table barely visible beneath the clutter of artist's debris sat beneath the window.

For a long moment Sean stared at the many paintings, seeing depth and feeling that only someone with great talent could capture.

One piece in particular arrested his gaze—a rendering of the coast viewed from out on the water. The landscape's bold strokes in various shades of blue, green and brown contrasted with the storm-clouded sky and revealed a passion as forceful as the crashing waves.

The piece would be magnificent once she finished painting it. As magnificent as the artist herself. He was finding he liked Lauren, liked the way her mouth quirked when she talked, liked her honest and forthright way of asking him questions and appreciated that though she was wary of him, a total stranger, she wasn't frightened of him when she had every right to be, considering the events of the evening. Distrust and fear could have easily overtaken her. But her willingness to depend on him, despite her initial reluctance, spoke to her strength of character. He admired that a great deal.

He retrieved the two small black carry-on suitcases from the closet and turned to leave. Again, his gaze strayed to the unfinished seascape.

Knowing he wouldn't be around to see the finished work struck him with a strange sense of melancholy.

Lauren braced herself for Sean's return, but when he didn't question her about the workroom, she relaxed as he helped her to her bedroom where her suitcases lay open on the bed.

"How can I help?" he asked.

She waved him away. "I can handle this on my own."

He bowed slightly before saying, "I'll go let the officers outside know the change in plans."

Alone in her room, she was tempted to sink onto her comforter and pretend she'd never left her bed this morning. Pretend that she hadn't been attacked on the beach—a horrifying event in itself—and that an attractive man hadn't entered her life, turning everything on end. She'd never met anyone like Sean. Right off the bat he cared—without knowing anything about her. Why would he do that? Could he really be a genuine Good Samaritan? She was sure there weren't many men like him in the world.

But the day had happened. She couldn't ignore

the events that had passed, good or bad. She already knew the past couldn't be changed. A lesson she'd learned five long years ago.

She wobbled to the dresser and stilled. Though the trinkets, jewelry box and small vase filled with dried flowers were where they should be, something seemed wrong. She studied the items but couldn't quite place what was bothering her. Was the box a little farther away from the wall than normal? Were the flowers arranged differently?

Chalking her unease up to more paranoia and fatigue, she quickly gathered necessities, along with a few more brightly colored sweat suits.

She'd given up wearing fashionable attire after the Nightmare. Her only nod to her old, eye-catching style was the colors she wore. If she were going to be a blob, she at least would be a colorful blob.

Sean appeared in the doorway. "You ready?"

"I just need a few things from the bathroom," she said.

With his help, she hobbled into the small space and froze as her gaze landed on the sink. She always kept her toothbrush holder on the left side of the faucet. Now it stood on the right side. Her gaze searched the room but she didn't see anything else out of place. Maybe she had moved the holder and hadn't realized she'd done so. It was possible. Wasn't it?

Suppressing a shudder, she grabbed her toiletries and stuck them in her suitcase. Sean came back to carry the cases out to the truck. As she hobbled into the living room, she paused and really looked around.

Was the picture on the mantel over the fireplace straighter than it had been before? Were her books on the shelf in the same order as when she'd last looked?

She quaked. This was getting ridiculous. She really was losing it. She needed some sleep.

Sean came back inside and bent to pick her up. Knowing how good it felt to be in his arms made her even more certain she shouldn't let herself enjoy it, so she hopped away. "I'll hobble out."

His mouth quirked. "Can I at least offer my arm?"

Okay, so she'd have to let him invade her bubble a little. "I'll need more than your arm. I'll need your whole side." She grinned back.

With a nod of acknowledgment, he slid his arm around her waist. She leaned into him as they slowly made their way to his waiting truck. Her ankle throbbed and she bit her lip. Stubbornness had a price.

Once in the passenger seat, she sat on her hands to keep from clenching them against the ache in her foot. She should have taken more pain medicine before trying to prove she wasn't totally helpless.

The interior of the truck smelled fresh and masculine. Like Sean. When he took his seat and drove toward town, she glanced at him, noting the strong lines of his straight nose and chiseled cheekbones.

A Christmas song played softly from the radio. She hummed along, marveling at how light in spirit she felt. There was something so soothing about being with Sean.

He turned the car onto Hemlock Street, Cannon Beach's main thoroughfare. Even on a cold December night, with a drizzling rain shrouding the hills, the town bustled as everyone prepared for Christmas.

Festive twinkling lights lit up the sidewalks, beckoning shoppers to wander in and out of the various unique stores. The four city blocks that made up Cannon Beach's commercial area were a mecca for photographers, artists and writers.

Lauren had always felt at home in the delightful town with its nooks, crannies and inviting paths leading to shops and galleries. She'd sat sketching in many of the garden courtyards when she'd first arrived at the beginning of summer.

The small-town ambiance and picturesque buildings of weathered cedar, their window boxes filled with winter blooms, brought peace to Lauren as they drove to the far end of Hemlock.

Sean drove the truck up a steep-inclined street, past cheerfully decorated cottages, then into an alley where he pulled up next to the cedar-sided, three-story house that had been converted into Shannon's Bed and Breakfast.

Turning off the engine, Sean slipped from the cab to open Lauren's door. Feeling safer than she had in five long years, she breathed in deeply the crisp winter air and allowed Sean to help her.

The Cannon Beach police cruiser pulled alongside them. Officer Kay rolled down his window. "This is a wise decision, Miss Curtis."

Lauren acknowledged his words with a nod. "You'll still be close though, right?"

"We'll drive through the neighborhood as often as possible. But honestly, I don't think you have anything to worry about. I doubt your attacker will return." Officer Kay saluted, rolled up the window and drove away.

Sean gave a wave as he led Lauren toward the door. They passed through an English-style garden, lush with evergreen foliage. An inviting brick patio welcomed them. Lauren couldn't wait to see the yard in daylight, though she could already imagine sipping tea and sitting beneath the magnolia tree in the summer, surrounded by flowering rosebushes and large hydrangea plants.

Sean opened the side door, which sported a wreath with a red bow, and revealed polished wooden floors reflecting moonlight streaming through the open door. To the right, through an arched doorway, she could make out a spacious and airy kitchen, with a center island that would undoubtedly be a gathering place for guests. Sean guided her down a short hall to a cozy reading alcove and helped her sit on a flower-upholstered chair. Light from wall sconces glowed over her right shoulder. Beneath her feet was a dark green patterned throw rug.

"I'll be right back," he said and darted back outside, leaving the door wide open.

A draft of frigid air blew in. A chill prickled her skin. A shadow flittered across the open doorway. "Sean?"

FOUR

"Hello."

Startled, Lauren yelped as she whipped around to see a tall, stately woman gliding down the hall toward her.

"Oh, dear, I didn't mean to startle you," the woman said as she stopped near Lauren where she sat. "You must be Lauren."

Catching her runaway breath, Lauren waved her hand. "Sorry. I'm a bit jumpy tonight. Yes, I'm Lauren."

"Mary Shannon." She stuck out her hand. "I'm so happy Sean was able to convince you to come stay with us after the fright you've had tonight."

Gripping the older woman's slender hand, Lauren immediately liked Mary's genuine smile and bright blue eyes that crinkled at the corners. Her red hair curled around an impish face, and her nautical-themed sweater and pants made Lauren feel as if she'd just stepped onto her yacht rather than into her home.

"Thank you for the offer," Lauren said, releasing Mary's hand.

"Let's get you situated in a room. I'll put you on the first floor so you don't have to navigate the stairs." Mary's eyes twinkled. "Though I'm sure Sean would be happy to be in charge of carrying you up and down."

Remembering how easily he'd lifted her into his arms heated Lauren's cheeks. She was saved from commenting by Sean, returning with her cases.

"I've made up the Mermaid Suite," Mary told him, waving a hand toward the hall.

With a grin, Sean headed that way.

"The Mermaid Suite?"

Pride gleamed in Mary's face. "Each room has a theme. It was such fun decorating them. I love the Pirate Room on the third floor the best. That's where Sean is staying."

"I'm not taking your room, am I?"

Mary laughed. "Oh, no. My room is down the hall from where you'll be."

With support from Mary, Lauren hobbled down the hall. Dried starfish and silk kelp clung to a fishing net draped on one wall. Pictures of the Oregon coast hung on the opposite wall. Sean stopped in front of a closed door, above which hung a small sign that read, The Mermaid.

Bracing herself for some garish display, Lauren peered inside. She was surprised and pleased to see the room didn't display tacky renditions of the mythical creatures. Rather, the room was done tastefully in shades of muted greens and white. The four-poster bed, covered with a sea of quilts and pillows, beckoned with comfort.

In the corner stood a two-foot-tall Christmas tree decorated with seashells and starfish ornaments. Next to the tree sat a plush sage-colored chair and ottoman and a floor lamp casting a soft light to illuminate the room. A window overlooked the garden. A perfect spot to read.

An antique white vanity with a gilded mirror beckoned with a display of trinkets from the sea. Sean set her suitcases on the floor.

"There's a private bath." Sean gestured past the matching dresser and sliding closet doors to a closed door.

"This is lovely," she remarked.

Mary beamed. "Can I help you get ready for bed?"

Lauren shook her head as she sank into the chair by the window. "I'll manage."

Nodding, Mary said, "Rest well, young lady.

We'll see you in the morning." Mary shooed Sean out before gliding from the room and quietly shutting the door behind her.

Lauren eased her head back and closed her eyes, grateful to Sean for his thoughtfulness for bringing her here. She was glad she hadn't allowed her stubbornness to keep her from accepting the invitation to stay here. Aunt Mary had such a welcoming way about her. Lauren really liked Mary. And Sean, too. She thought back to their conversation in the truck. When she'd asked him about church—a look of such utter sadness had flashed across his face. She'd wanted to ask what was wrong, but then they'd arrived at her house and the moment passed.

A line of scripture floated into her consciousness. "Bear one another's burdens, and thus fulfill the law of Christ."

What burdens did Sean carry?

"I can't bear any more burdens, Lord," she whispered.

A loud bang jarred Lauren awake. She jerked upright, the bedding impeding her movements, causing pain to shoot up her leg from her ankle.

She groaned and a shiver of apprehension tightened her shoulders. Shrouded in darkness, she strained to listen.

What had she heard? An intruder? Someone trying to get in through the window?

Her mind flashed to the horrible night that had changed her life. She'd been alone then, too. Her attacker had jimmied a window and silently entered her studio. But she'd survived. Barely.

Helplessness and vulnerability swamped her. Terror set off alarms through her mind.

No, wait.

Memory flooded in. She wasn't alone. She was safe in Shannon's Bed and Breakfast with Sean and Mary. Releasing the hold she had on the soft comforter, she took several deep breaths.

Rain batted against the windows. Thunder rolled through the night.

A crash of thunder must have been what she'd heard.

She was panicking for nothing.

Letting out a sigh of relief, she settled back against the fluffy pillows and tried not to shiver with residual fear. Storms didn't usually bother her, but tonight the dark seemed oppressive and the howling wind outside fueled her imagination.

Between the attack on the beach and the scare at the hospital, it was no wonder she was jumpy.

But she wouldn't have to relive the Nightmare again. Adrian Posar was securely locked up in prison, where he'd never be able to hurt her again. The police would find the beach attacker and all would be well.

Closing her eyes, Lauren forced her mind to concentrate on a blank canvas. She fell back to sleep with a sketch of Sean's handsome face etched in her mind, even as a lingering sense of dread gripped her heart.

Morning came with a rush of sunlight gliding into the room. Lauren opened her eyes and stared at the scene above her. A mural of frolicking mer-people in a blue and green sea covered the ceiling. She hadn't noticed the painting last night. With a critical eye she assessed the work. Not bad. Some of the proportions were off, but painting upside down had to be a difficult feat so she decided to just enjoy the view.

Turning her head, she glanced at the side-table clock. Her eyes widened. It was almost noon. She couldn't remember the last time she'd slept in so late. The cushy bed cradled her body, the comforter kept the December chill out, making it far too easy to sleep deeply. Even now, she didn't want to leave the safety and warmth of the bed.

But laziness wasn't acceptable. With a soft groan, she rolled to her good side and then slid her feet from beneath the covers to land on the floor.

Gingerly, she tested her foot. Her ankle throbbed. She shifted all her weight to her uninjured leg.

Dressing and using the facilities proved exhausting, but she hadn't wanted to ask for help. By the time she emerged from her room, sweat trickled down her neck and she was shaking. The hallway was empty. A distinct pounding from above told her Sean was working. She contemplated calling for him, but decided she could make it to the kitchen on her own steam.

She hobbled down the hall, using the wall for support. When she entered the beautifully appointed kitchen, she found Mary Shannon at the stove. Today she wore another nautical-themed outfit in yellows and blue. She even sported tassels on the hem of her sweater.

"Good morning," Lauren said, though her voice sounded winded.

Mary whipped around, a hand going to the base of her throat. "Oh, my. This time you startled me." She smiled and wiped her hands on a towel. "Did you sleep well?"

"Very," Lauren replied as she eased into a cane-back chair at the breakfast nook table. "You?"

"I kept hearing noises. Must have been the weather," Mary stated. Concern flashed in her delicately-lined face. "You don't look so good."

Lauren didn't feel so good. Nausea roiled in her empty stomach. She needed food and more painkillers. "Could I bother you for something to eat? I shouldn't take my medication on an empty stomach."

"No bother at all," Mary said. "I was just fixing Sean's lunch. Seafood gumbo." A frown furrowed her brow. "It's a bit spicy. Would you care for some? Or would you like something a little milder?"

Though the gumbo smelled delicious, Lauren wasn't sure she could do spicy. "Milder, please."

"Eggs and toast?"

"Perfect." Lauren tried to rise from the chair. "Let me help."

"Nonsense," Mary scolded. "You're my guest and you're injured. You sit, relax. Food will be up in a jiffy."

"Thank you." Lauren sat back down, grateful to take the pressure off her foot. Overhead, she heard a power saw start up. "It was nice of Sean to move here to help you with your renovations."

Carrying a plate of fluffy eggs and buttered toast to the table, Mary nodded. "Yes. It's been good for him to be here. He needed a change."

"Is he a carpenter by trade?"

A slight smile tugged at the corners of Mary's lips. "That's a question you'll have to ask him."

She'd tried, but he'd sidestepped the question, turning the conversation back on her. Interesting. She ate the meal and took her medication. By the time Sean entered the kitchen for his lunch, she was drowsy again. And didn't even protest when he carried her back to her room and tucked her back in bed.

As she drifted off, she felt the soft touch of a kiss on her forehead. She smiled and surrendered to sleep.

Night fell with a fresh winter storm coming ashore. The windows rattled with gale winds barreling off the ocean and rain tapping on the glass. As far as Sean was concerned, it was a perfect night for a cozy fire, hot chocolate, Christmas music and a beautiful woman by his side. Lauren.

All day, he'd been looking forward to spending a relaxed evening with her. Hoping to get to know her better. So far he really liked her. Liked her kind and warm-hearted nature when she wasn't watching him with wariness in her pretty eyes.

After a dinner of clam chowder, bread and fresh green salad, Sean, Lauren and Aunt Mary moved to the living room. Sean noticed how much more animated and lively Lauren had become throughout the course of the afternoon. She'd slept for another couple of hours before venturing out of her room again.

At one point, when he'd come down for a bottle of water, he'd found the two women chatting away about color schemes and accessories for the rooms he was working on. Somewhere Aunt Mary had found a crutch for Lauren to use. And later, when he'd stopped for the day, he'd discovered them bent over a jigsaw puzzle laid out on the game table in the parlor.

He'd known Lauren would be a good distraction for his aunt and his aunt a good distraction for Lauren. He just hadn't thought someone as obviously wary as Lauren would bond so soon. Aunt Mary had a way of making people feel welcome.

He wished Lauren would loosen up with him, as well. Earning her trust was becoming very important to him, though he couldn't pinpoint why.

He sat in a wingback chair close to the warmth of the stone gas fireplace, sipping from a large mugful of cocoa. The day's newspaper lay next to him waiting to be read. Colorful lights danced on the tree near the front window.

Lauren left the puzzle and, using the crutch, hobbled over to a matching chair next to him, while Mary settled across from them on a small love seat, tucking a blanket around her legs.

"Tell us what it was like growing up in Hollywood," Mary said.

Sean sat forward. Lauren had opened up that much to Aunt Mary? Being from Hollywood was more telling than just L.A.

A pensive smile touched Lauren's lips. "Did you ever see the early-nineties TV show *90210?*"

Mary shook her head. "I've never been big on television."

"I've seen the reruns and the newer version," Sean offered, thinking of the young and beautiful teens full of angst, navigating high school in a world of wealth and privilege. A world foreign to him. He'd grown up in a middle-class suburb of Portland, full of soccer moms and working dads. He and his siblings had had their share of teen issues—finding the right crowd, having a limited budget for clothes. Certainly having a car was out of the question especially since they lived two blocks from the high school—but nothing as dramatic as what the TV show portrayed.

"I grew up in that same zip code, but my experience was nothing like the show, even though my father was a movie producer. I lived in a middle class part of town."

Sean figured even middle class Hollywood was more affluent than the suburb he'd grown up in.

Lauren didn't appear pretentious at all. Another reason to admire her.

Mary's eyes widened with interest. "Ooh, swanky."

Lauren's mouth quirked. "He and my mother met on a movie set. She was an extra with stars in her eyes for fame and glory. She chose being the wife of an up-and-coming movie mogul over pursuing her own career. But when I was three, Dad left her for a younger starlet." She smiled grimly. "Such a cliché."

Sean's heart ached for the pain he could tell she was trying to hide. Her father's desertion of his family had left a wound on her soul. From his experience working with teens, Sean had seen firsthand how devastating an absent father could be on a child. It was always worse when the father remarried and cleaved to his new family, leaving his children to suffer heartbreak.

Remembering Lauren's comment about her father being dead, he asked, "When did he die?"

"A few years later in a skiing accident in Colorado. From then on it was just Mom and me."

"And she still lives in Los Angeles?" Mary asked gently.

"Yes. Dad had a big life insurance policy and thankfully, since he hadn't remarried, the money came to us. Mom still had to work, though. When she couldn't book consistent acting gigs, she became an agent. She owns her own agency now."

Lauren exchanged a glance with Sean. "Though at the moment she's on a cruise. She'll be back in time for Christmas day."

"How nice for her," Mary said. "I've always wanted to cruise the Caribbean."

"You know, Aunt Mary, if you ever want to go on a vacation, I'd be willing to run the place for you," Sean interjected.

Giving her nephew a thoughtful look, Mary replied, "I just might take you up on that, once the rooms are done." Mary turned her gaze to Lauren. "Sean tells me you are quite an artist. I would love some fresh pieces for the living room and dining room."

Lauren paled. "I—I don't sell my work."

"You could, though," Sean stated. "You've got the talent, for sure. And I saw several canvasses in your workroom that would work well here if you finished them."

Dropping her gaze to her folded hands resting on her lap, Lauren muttered, "I don't paint anymore."

"I don't understand. Why would you walk away from such a wonderful gift?"

"It's complicated," she said, her eyes flashing with emotion. Hurt, anger? Or was that fear?

A lump formed in his chest. He reached out to cover her clenched hands. What could possibly have frightened her enough to make her stop painting?

Lauren swallowed, unsure how to explain. She hated the question. Hated the answer even more. The Nightmare.

"Sean, dear, obviously this is upsetting to Lauren. Let us tell you what we planned for the third room upstairs," Mary said.

Grateful for the change in subject, Lauren relaxed as she and Mary explained their ideas. An hour later, Mary tossed the blanket aside and rose. "Children, I'm off to bed."

"'Night, Aunt Mary," Sean said.

"Good night," Lauren said. "Thank you again for allowing me to stay here."

"My pleasure, dear. You stay as long as you want. I really enjoy having some female company," Mary said before gliding from the room.

"Would you like some more cocoa?" Sean asked.

Lauren held up her hand, palm out. "No. If I drink any more, I definitely won't sleep tonight."

Sean leaned forward to stoke the fire. The warm glow of the dancing flames touched his hair, highlighting the dark auburn and bathing his strong features. Lauren suppressed a sigh. She couldn't remember the last time she'd spent such a relaxing evening.

Sean sat back and pinned her with his blue eyes. "Lauren, why haven't you finished any of your oil paintings?"

She sucked in a breath at the repeated question. So much for relaxing. "I told you, it's complicated."

"You obviously have a lot of talent. It seems a shame to let those pieces of half-finished art sit in a room collecting dust."

She shook her head. "I just…"

Did she dare tell him the truth? Then she'd have to tell him everything, things she hadn't talked about in a long time, and then only with her therapist. She stared into his eyes, wanting to trust him like she hadn't trusted anyone since that awful night.

The need to talk became a burden. One that pressed on her heart.

"Can I consider you a friend?" she asked,

needing to know they both understood the boundaries of their relationship, boundaries she doubted either of them wanted to cross.

His intense regard made her want to squirm. She held herself still, waiting. It was clear he wanted to hold back. She didn't blame him. He had seen enough of her scars to know what he was committing himself to.

But he gave a nod and her heartbeat sped up.

"Five years ago something…bad happened." She nervously watched his face. "I was attacked."

Shock and distress etched lines in Sean's face. "Who attacked you?"

She shook her head, not sure she should continue. Because if she did, there would be no turning back.

Sean leaned over to take her hands in his. The newspaper slipped to the floor. "Who did this to you?"

"A man named Adrian Posar."

Just saying his name aloud brought back a rush of terror, shuddering down her spine. Taking a deep breath, she slowly exhaled and then continued. "I was working late in my studio when he broke in. The police said he entered through a back window, as was his M.O."

Sean's face paled. "He'd done it before?"

She nodded. "He was a serial rapist plaguing Westwood, where I lived."

Sean jerked in reaction, but she clung to his hand and forced herself to continue. "He'd raped and killed four other women. The police were sure he picked the women randomly. Maybe watched them for a day or so before making his move. Me, I worked most nights in the studio after my employees left. I was an easy target, I guess." She let out a self-deprecating scoff. "Just like last night."

Sean squeezed her hand. She could see how upset this was making him. She considered stopping but it was too late. "When he attacked me, we struggled. A candle was knocked over. Paint solvent spilled and ignited. We were both burned in the fire."

Sean closed his eyes briefly as if in pain. His eyes jerked open. "The assailant last night wasn't…?"

"No," she assured him quickly. "I thought so at first, but Adrian Posar's in prison."

"That's—that's a relief," he said. "But then, who was that guy last night?"

With a shrug, she replied, "Random, I guess."

She stared at the dancing flames in the fireplace. It had taken her two years before she could bear to even see a fire, let alone sit close enough to feel the warmth.

For a moment silence stretched between them.

"How bad is the scarring?" Sean finally asked, his voice so soft, so tender she wanted to cry.

His rapt attention never strayed as she told him of the grueling treatment in the burn center, the grafting and painful process of physical therapy. When she ran out of words, she wiped at the stray tears streaming down her cheeks. "I've never understood what I did to deserve this."

Sean took her other hand, his palms warm and comforting. "Lauren, what happened was not your fault."

His gentle but firm rebuke stirred her anger. "But why did God allow it? He's in control. I know that. So why didn't He prevent the Nightmare?"

Her words tumbled out before she realized what she was saying. She felt guilty for voicing the questions that plagued her.

"We don't always understand God's ways. I'm sure there's some purpose."

Rage nearly choked her. "What possible purpose could this serve?" She waved a hand down her side.

"Sometimes things happen so that we might learn to trust, not in ourselves, but in God." Sean's patient voice soothed some of her ire. "Like the

Apostle Paul, we might learn to be content in every circumstance."

Disbelief clouded her vision. "So you're saying I had a lesson to learn? That God used the attack as a means to teach me something?"

She didn't like what that said about her. Or God. She'd been told all her life that God was a loving God. And she'd always thought she had trusted God, but…Sean squeezed her hand, drawing her attention.

"No, I don't think God condoned this madman's actions. But God does give us, *all of us,* free will."

"He shouldn't give evil people free will," she said, her voice thick with anger.

"If only it were that simple." He lifted her chin with his hand until their gazes met. "I know God wept with you. But I also firmly believe God has a plan for your life. And He uses our circumstances for good. Even the bad circumstances. Have you ever heard the story of Queen Ester?"

"Of course." Ester's story was a biblical fairy tale. A beautiful commoner became a queen, saved her people and won the love of the king. What little girl wouldn't love that story? But Lauren wasn't a child anymore.

"Her life, her rise to royalty, culminated in one

great opportunity to serve God. Your life and this tragic event might be used one day to serve God."

A cynical scoff escaped her. "How?"

"Only God can reveal His intent to you, but you must be open and willing to listen to Him. He loves you. You are His child."

She knew Sean meant well. And she wanted to believe his words. But too much anger, too much cynicism had built up around her heart.

Tilting her head to one side, she searched his face. "You should be a pastor or counselor or something. You're very good. Have you ever thought of changing careers?"

Pain flashed in his eyes. "I—" He shook his head, as if telling himself not to speak. His expression turned distant and she could feel his emotional withdrawal acutely as he released her hands. "It's late. You should really rest. I'll assist you to your room."

A little hurt and confused by the chasm forming between them, she allowed him to help her to her feet and took his arm for support. A quick glance at his face revealed his tight jaw and shadowed eyes. Why wouldn't he talk about himself? What was he hiding?

Despite everything, a yearning for the evening

to continue tugged at her heart. She wanted to find out more about Sean, but obviously he had no intention of sharing himself with her. She shouldn't be surprised. She wasn't a permanent fixture in his life. His duty to her would soon be over. She had to remember her resolve not to become attached to Sean—there would only be hurt and sorrow down that road. She'd had enough of both to last several lifetimes.

Fumbling with her crutch, she took a hobbled step forward and nearly slipped on the newspaper beneath her feet. She glanced down and froze. The headline on the *Cannon Beach Daily* blazed before her eyes. Her breath seized in her chest.

California Prison Fire. One Officer Dead. Inmate Escapes.

Clutching Sean's arm with one hand, Lauren pointed to the paper and choked out, "What does the rest of the headline story say?"

Sean bent to retrieve the newsprint. His eyes widened as he read the article. When he lifted his gaze, she sucked in a panicked breath at the horror clouding the blue of his eyes.

"Adrian Posar has escaped."

FIVE

"Lauren, I've been trying to reach you for hours," Detective Jarvis said in a voice grave with concern.

Lauren tightened her hold on the receiver. After seeing the jarring news article, Sean had helped her into the kitchen where she'd used the phone to call the detective. Her heart slammed against her ribs like a bird trying to escape a cage. "Is it true? Did he escape?"

"Unfortunately, yes."

A tidal wave of horror crashed over her, knocking the breath from her lungs and sending her mind reeling. Her worst fears had been confirmed.

"Where are you staying? I'll have the police there in Cannon Beach come get you," the detective said.

"I'm safe for now." Anxiety twisted in the pit of her stomach. "But it would be good if you alerted them. They need to know who they're dealing with." She quickly told him of the attack on the beach and the scare at the hospital. She wasn't crazy. Not this time. This time her worst fears had materialized.

"I don't know how he found out where you are or how he managed to get up there so quickly," Jarvis said in a voice harsh with rage.

How could God let this happen again? Fresh fear and anger converged to create a toxic mixture bubbling in her veins. She tried to think, to formulate a plan. She had to leave. Now, before Adrian attacked again. Next time, she might not be so blessed as to have Sean rescue her.

"I have to leave. I have to go someplace where he can't find me," she said into the phone, as tension built in her chest, making her ache.

"I don't think that's a good idea. He could be watching you right now, waiting for you to be alone. He'd only follow you. Stay put. I'll have the police camp outside your door."

"I'm not at my house," she told him. "I'm at a friend's."

And she was putting Sean and his aunt in jeopardy by being here. Dismay throbbed at her temple. She'd hate for anything to happen to these nice people who'd taken her in and shown her such kindness. "Maybe the police should take me home."

"No!" Sean said from behind her.

She whipped her head around to look at him. "But I'm putting you and Mary in danger."

"You'll be in more danger alone. You can't physically fight him or run from him with your injured foot. You're staying here," Sean stated, his voice firm.

Her heart squeezed tight. She wanted to put her trust, her life in Sean's hands, but did she dare? If anything happened to him or Mary, she'd never forgive herself.

"I agree, Lauren," came Detective Jarvis's voice over the line. "I doubt Posar will try anything as long as you're with other people. He's a coward at heart."

A viselike band of dread squeezed her around the middle. "I hope you're right," she said. "I'll stay here."

"Good. I need the phone number and address. I'll be on the next plane out of L.A. I want to nail Posar to the wall."

Glad to hear the detective would come, Lauren handed the phone over to Sean so he could give Jarvis the needed information.

"Don't worry. I'm not about to let anything happen to her," Sean said before hanging up the phone.

Guilt for burdening Sean with her trouble weighed heavily on her heart. She laid a hand on his arm. "Thank you."

He covered her hand with his, the pressure sure and warm. "I made a promise to take care of you. I don't renege on my promises. Besides, we have God on our side."

Tears of gratefulness burned the back of her eyes. Sean was a man of honor and integrity. A man who kept his promises. She could only hope his promise didn't get him or Mary killed.

Sean dragged one of the wingback chairs from the living room into the hall and stationed himself outside Lauren's room. Light from the wall sconce reflected off the baseball bat lying at his feet. No one was getting past him to Lauren. He would protect her with everything in him.

Life had certainly taken a left turn since yesterday. He'd come to Cannon Beach to escape the memories of his past. Working on the renovations for Aunt Mary, he'd been able to keep his hands busy, forcing his mind to concentrate on the work rather than on what couldn't be undone. But that all changed with the decision to run on the beach.

When he'd gone jogging last night, he'd never expected to end up rescuing a beautiful woman from a madman, let alone bring her home with him to protect her.

And hearing the heartbreaking details of her story made his own heart ache with compassion and sympathy. And anger. Anger at the monster who'd brought this undeserved horrible tragedy upon Lauren. And others. Sean's stomach rolled at the thought of the poor victims who hadn't lived through their ordeal with the same man. Sean could only hope their pain had ended quickly.

But for Lauren, though she had physically survived the brutal attacks five years ago and yesterday, she was emotionally wounded. The attacks had damaged her trust in people, but there had been other sorrows, as well.

Those caused by her father, first from his abandoning the family, then by his death. Sean couldn't imagine how hard that had been. His own father was a rock, a good man Sean looked up to. Collin Matthews was the anchor that held their family together. Sean couldn't bear the thought of anything happening to him. Or his mother. Guilt for leaving them so abruptly nagged at him. He needed to make things right between them, make sure they knew his departure from his former life had nothing to do with them.

And everything to do with his own failure.

But he wouldn't fail Lauren.

Tonight, he'd so wanted to help her, to guide her toward God's healing love. While he knew she was a believer, her pain and sadness were blocking her from the true peace that faith could offer. For a moment he'd allowed himself to reach out, to do what he'd been trained to do—guide her with words of wisdom, words of scripture, to a better understanding of God and faith to a place of healing.

And she'd called him on it, intelligently surmising he was more than he seemed. She was not only beautiful, but perceptive and honest. A potent combination.

He wasn't a pastor. But he was a trained guidance counselor. Using his education combined with his faith to guide teens at a high school had been his passion. Until tragedy had struck.

His hands fisted. He wasn't going to let disaster strike here. He'd failed six months ago to prevent a tragedy, a life lost, but here, with Lauren, he would keep her safe and protected.

He'd made a promise to Dr. Sorensen to care for Lauren. The request had been of necessity because of her injury. Now, she needed him to guard her life. To show her a way to healing her soul.

He'd just have to remember to protect his heart as well.

* * *

The next morning, Lauren awoke just as the first faint fingers of dawn crept over the winter-gray horizon. She felt frazzled from a night spent tossing and turning, every little noise making her jumpy. She threw the covers off and dressed as quickly as she could with her bum ankle.

She didn't want to disturb Mary or Sean, so she stayed in her room for another hour, trying to read from a book she'd discovered in one of the dresser drawers, but the biography of a past president didn't hold her attention.

Instead, she found herself staring out the window at the cloudy sky and at the top of a police car parked just on the other side of the fence. Obviously, Detective Jarvis had contacted the Cannon Beach police. She wondered if the same two officers who'd met her at the hospital now sat outside in the frosty morning air.

When finally she couldn't take another moment holed up in the room, she opened her bedroom door and found Sean blinking at her from where he sat in a chair in the hall. Surprised pleasure tingled through her. Finding any other guy camped outside her door would have creeped her out, but there was something about Sean that made her feel safe and treasured.

His dark auburn hair was tousled as if he'd run his fingers through the thick waves. He smiled and stretched his long limbs. Lauren's pulse picked up. Lanky but graceful, Sean emitted a vital energy that crackled in the air.

Swallowing heavily as heat crept up her neck, she said, "Good morning. Did you sit here awake all night?"

He rose. "I did."

Affection for his chivalrous protection unfurled in her chest. "Did you know there's a police car outside?"

His mouth lifted at one corner. "Good to know. I'll take some coffee out to them. Are you hungry?"

Her stomach was tied up in knots. "Not really."

Peering at her with concern, he said, "You need to keep up your strength."

She couldn't argue with his logic. "Then I guess I should try to eat."

Nodding with satisfaction, he gestured down the hall. "After you."

Using the crutch for support, she made her way to the kitchen. "What can I do to help?"

Waving her toward the table, he said, "I've got it. Toast, coffee, eggs. Nothing spectacular."

"That sounds perfect." She sat and leaned the crutch against the wall. Her gaze strayed out the picture window into the fenced-off garden.

Beyond the perimeter of the fence, a white utility van pulled to a stop. A worker exited the vehicle, hitched his tool belt over his navy coveralls and moved to a telephone pole. A white hardhat covered his head, and a thick beard and mustache protected his exposed skin from the chilly air. She watched as he climbed the metal rungs going up the side of the utility pole. She shivered. She certainly wouldn't want that job.

"Here we go," Sean said as he set a plate of light and airy scrambled eggs in front of her, along with two pieces of sliced buttered toast and a mug of fresh brewed coffee.

"Thank you." She picked up her fork and took a bite. Her stomach growled. The knot in her stomach eased slightly, making her conscious of her hunger. When he sat down with his own breakfast, she asked, "What brought you to Cannon Beach?"

He raised an eyebrow. "Aunt Mary needed my help."

After swallowing the bite she'd just taken, she said, "I get a sense it was more than that. Mary said you needed a change."

He raised an eyebrow. "Did she, now? Well, sometimes we all need a change."

An evasive parry, if ever there was one. She tried a different tract. "How long have you been a carpenter?"

He shrugged and finished off his eggs and toast before scooting his chair back. He stood and cleared the plates, setting them in the sink. She stared. Why was he so reluctant to talk about himself? He'd said he was her friend, so why was he closing himself off from her?

"I know there's a thermos here somewhere," he said as he searched through the cupboards.

"Why do you keep doing that?"

He found a thermal carafe and poured coffee into it. "Doing what?"

Curiosity nipped at her. "Avoid talking about yourself. I'd like to get to know you better."

"I don't see the point. It won't help," he said and reached for the kitchen door handle.

She tucked in her chin as hurt slammed into her. Memories rose, assaulting in their intensity. Greg had said something similar just before he'd walked out of her life. He hadn't seen the point in a relationship with her when he couldn't stand the sight of her scars. She hadn't thought that Sean was cut of the same cloth, but obviously he was.

Sean paused to peer at her in concern. "You okay?"

Obviously, her expression gave away her inner feelings. She tried to school her features into nonchalance. "Sure, why wouldn't I be?"

His eyebrows drew together. "Look, I just don't like talking about myself. There are some things better left alone."

"That's fine. I get it. There's no point in opening up to me when I'll be out of your life soon enough."

It was a mistake staying here. She was damaged goods, a burden. As soon as Detective Jarvis arrived she'd have him take her someplace else. She rose unsteadily to stand and tested her weight on her bad ankle. Though still painful, she could bear more weight this morning. She reached for the crutch. It slipped from her grasp and landed with a bang on the floor.

Sean moved to her side. He set the thermos on the table and then placed his hands on her shoulders. "Lauren, that's not what I mean."

She met his gaze. "Then what did you mean?"

He blew out a breath, looking contrite. "I guess I have been using avoidance tactics. I'm sorry. It has nothing to do with you."

"Then what does your avoidance have to do with?"

Raw, primitive pain flashed in his blue eyes. Something or someone had hurt him.

Her heart acknowledged his pain, and compassion filled her. She slipped her arms around his waist. "Whatever it is, you can tell me."

He tucked a strand of her hair behind her ear. "Your life is in danger. You shouldn't have to be burdened with my troubles when you have your own to deal with."

Reminded of her Nightmare, she quaked. "It's freaking me out that he's on the loose."

He hugged her close. "I can totally understand that. But you can't let the fear win."

She gave a bitter laugh. "It already has. It's taken so much from me."

He leaned back to look at her face, his expression so tender, so distressed on her behalf. "You mean your painting?"

He was too perceptive for her comfort. "Yes. Among other things." Her self-esteem. Her ability to trust.

He raised a questioning eyebrow.

No way would she disclose how ugly and unlovable she felt. She couldn't take seeing confirmation of those feelings or pity in his eyes. The silence stretched, pulling at her already taut nerves. She dropped her gaze.

"I think you should start painting again," he said softly.

Dismayed, her gaze snapped to his face. "I can't."

A gentle smile curved his lips. "You can."

Agitation beat through her system like the delicate wings of a butterfly. Paint again? Longing swamped her. Yet a yawning terror sucked it away. The thought of picking up a paintbrush and reaching into the place of creativity that had been invaded and violated by violence and rage left her frozen, immobile to act, to create with color. Her world was now shades of black and white, like her charcoal sketches.

She shuddered and gave a negative shake of her head. "No."

"I'll help you."

She blinked. This man was such a puzzle to her. So generous yet so closed off. And here he'd done it again, skillfully avoided revealing anything of himself and turning the focus back on her. "Why would you want to help me?"

"Because I believe in you, in your talent. You have a God-given gift that shouldn't be wasted."

His words warmed her soul. But the fear wouldn't let go.

"Finish just one painting," he coaxed.

Again the desire to paint, to hold a brush and create beauty on a canvas, overwhelmed her and throbbed like an ache much worse than the pain in her injured ankle. If Sean handled the flammable materials…if she made sure no candles or anything else with a flame were nearby…if she was careful…if she didn't breathe in…

Could she tap into her creativity and not let the smell of paint, the feel of the brush in her hand thrust her mind back to the Nightmare? Was she strong enough? Only one way to find out. Slowly, she nodded.

The smile of approval and joy on Sean's face tugged at her heart. Why was her success at conquering her fear so important to him?

Sean grabbed a pad of paper and a pen from a drawer and handed them to her. "Make a list of what you need and I'll go pick it up from your cottage."

"I can go," she said, her mind inventorying all the necessary items.

He shook his head. "Too dangerous. You have to stay here, inside the house. I'll bring everything to you."

Knowing he was right didn't make accepting his words any easier. She didn't like being cooped up, but what choice did she have? She quickly made a list with instructions on where to find the items.

When he left with the list in one hand and the thermos in the other, she made her way back to her room. Second thoughts assailed her. Could she do it? Could she paint again?

Or would the fear win?

You have a God-given gift that shouldn't be wasted.

She'd always thought of her art as God inspired. Lifting her eyes heavenward, she whispered, "Help me, please."

For now, that was as much as she could ask for.

Perched near the top of the telephone pole behind Shannon's Bed and Breakfast, Adrian had a bird's-eye view into the place. The cops sitting in the car just yards away were oblivious to his presence. They saw what he'd wanted them to see. Just some blue-collar worker making a living.

It would be hours, if not days, before anyone missed the utility truck or its rightful driver, who was right now unconscious and tied up inside the windowless van. It had been a stroke of luck to have stumbled upon the guy last night at the hospital when Adrian had followed Lauren there.

Too bad all he'd managed to do last night was injure her foot and give her a little scare in the radiology room. It had cost him money he really couldn't spare to bribe the orderly to bring her there, but it had been worth it—far better than just the pleasure of knowing he must have frightened her with the way he'd poked around her house, rearranging her possessions.

Anger seethed in Adrian's soul as he watched Lauren blithely eating and chatting with that man, the jogger, as if she hadn't a care in the world. Obviously, her life hadn't been ruined, like she'd ruined his.

Adrian's teeth gnashed at his scarred lips, the deadened flesh thick and rubbery. The coppery taste of blood where he broke the skin filled his mouth. He spat it out.

Soon, very soon, there would be an opportunity. A moment would present itself when she was alone and then she'd know what real terror meant. It would only be a matter of time. Adrian had learned patience in prison. And many other useful things that he would show to Lauren once he had her to himself. And no jogger was going to interfere.

He pretended to work on the telephone lines,

but was in reality setting up a small camera to monitor Lauren's movements and feed the video to a laptop computer inside the van. He'd learned the ins and outs of video surveillance while in the joint. Amazing how much information could be gleaned off the Internet during his computer access time. Procuring the necessary items hadn't been difficult. Not for a man like him. Breaking and entering, taking what he wanted was as natural as breathing.

Jogger-man exited the house and stopped beside the police car at the end of the driveway to hand the cops a silver thermos, before climbing into a black truck and driving away.

Swinging his gaze back to the house, Adrian saw Lauren enter her bedroom. Her curtains were open just enough for him to see her crawl to the middle of the bed and draw her knees to her chest.

Adrian's breath quickened with anticipation.

Maybe his opportunity was now.

SIX

A loud knock echoed through the stillness of the bed-and-breakfast. Startled by the sudden noise, Lauren tensed. Had Sean forgotten his key? Slipping from the bed, she limped to the bedroom door. She opened it and peered into the hall. Mary walked toward the front door.

"Wait," Lauren called out.

Mary halted and blinked at Lauren. Today, her red hair was swept up in a topknot and she wore tailored navy slacks, a kelly-green, long-sleeved blouse with ruffles at the neckline and cuffs and a bright smile—until she caught sight of Lauren's expression.

Rushing as best she could with a throbbing foot to Mary's side, Lauren said, "It might not be safe."

Concern marred Mary's forehead as her eyebrows drew together. "Safe? What's going on?"

Guilt for bringing danger to this kind woman's

home twisted inside Lauren's gut. "It's a long story. One I will tell you later."

The loud rap of knuckles on the wooden door shuddered through Lauren. She glanced at the door. Sean? Or…would Adrian knock? Did monsters keep to such civility?

Cautiously, Lauren approached the door and peered through the peephole. She recognized the man on the other side and let out a relieved breath. She wrenched the door open. "Detective Jarvis, please come in."

The older man stepped inside. He was tall, with hair the color of salt and pepper, shorn close to his head on the sides and left a little longer on the top. His pale blue eyes always seeming to take everything in. "You okay?"

Lauren offered him a smile. "Yes, thank you. Detective, this is Mary Shannon, my hostess. Mary, this is…" How did she explain him? "This is Detective Nate Jarvis of the LAPD."

Lauren noted the flare of interest in his gaze as he held out his hand.

"Good of you to take Lauren in," he said.

Mary stepped forward and grasped his outstretched hand. "There's always room here for those in need. And being that it's Christmastime, it's only fitting to offer shelter and comfort."

"I'm sure this isn't the way any of us would like to spend Christmas," he replied.

"What brings you to Cannon Beach then?" Mary asked.

Jarvis cast Lauren an inquiring glance.

"I haven't explained everything yet," Lauren said.

"Ah. Is Mr. Matthews here?" Jarvis asked.

"Sean went to my cottage to get something," Lauren explained.

Jarvis frowned. "Not a good idea. He could lead Posar back here."

Contrite, Lauren grimaced. "We didn't think of that."

"I have his cell number. Should we call him?" Mary asked.

Jarvis nodded with approval at Mary. "Yes."

Mary led the way to the kitchen, where she picked up the phone, dialed and waited for Sean to answer.

As Mary and then Jarvis talked with Sean, Lauren's gaze went to the window. The telephone guy and his van were gone.

Jarvis hung up the phone. "Mr. Matthews will take a roundabout way coming back."

"Detective, would you like a cup of coffee while you and Lauren fill me in on what is going on?"

Mary smiled sweetly, but her determined gaze stated she wanted answers.

Jarvis inclined his head. "Coffee sounds great." To Lauren he said, "Have you heard from your mother? I went by her place but she wasn't there."

"She's on a cruise but said she'd be back in time to celebrate Christmas with me here."

"Considering Christmas Eve is only three days away, let's pray we catch Posar before then."

Lauren's mouth went dry. Three days. Could they find him by then? Would God make it happen? Did she dare hope?

They moved to the kitchen and sat at the dining table while they told Mary the story. When they were done, Mary sat back with a stunned expression. "Oh, you poor dear. The attack at the beach was horrible enough, but this… Thank God above He sent Sean out jogging the other night."

Lauren couldn't have agreed more. Even though God hadn't stopped Adrian from coming after her, He at least provided her with some protection. That was definitely something to be grateful for. And now Detective Jarvis was here.

"I've alerted the local law enforcement agencies all up and down the coast to be on the lookout for Posar. He can't stay hidden for long. Someone will spot his scarred face and then we'll be able to catch him."

"How did he manage to escape?" Mary asked.

Lauren wondered the same thing.

"He's a wily man," Jarvis said. "The arson investigators are pretty sure the blaze started in one of the supply closets in the prison infirmary. Apparently, Adrian had been complaining of stomach issues so he'd been taken to see the doc. He was left alone long enough to start the blaze.

"When all was said and done, a charred body with Posar's ID tags was found. It wasn't until later that the warden realized one of his guards was missing. Witnesses said they saw a guard walk out of the prison yard. When the crime-scene lab compared the missing guard's dental records with the dead man's, they matched."

Mary's complexion drained of color. "That's just so awful."

Anguished to have put Mary in such a precarious position, Lauren reached over to take her hand. "He's a monster. I think I should leave, return to my own house or maybe leave town. My presence here only puts you and Sean in jeopardy."

Clearly affronted by the suggestion, Mary said, "Nonsense. You're by far safer here."

"I agree," Jarvis stated firmly. "Staying with

other people is the smartest thing to do while I beat the bushes for him."

Touched that he would put so much of himself into ending her nightmare made tears burn the back of her eyelids. Gratitude clogged her throat.

"Do you have a place to stay?" Mary asked the detective.

"Not yet. I came straight here," Jarvis answered.

"Then you'll stay here, as well," Mary said. "We have plenty of rooms and you can keep us all safe."

Jarvis's blue eyes widened for a moment, then his expression settled into resolve. "I'll take you up on that offer."

Mary beamed. "Wonderful. I'll go make up the Captain's Quarters."

When she left the room, Jarvis turned to Lauren. "Nice lady."

Sensing there was more than just politeness in his observation, she grinned. "Yes. And she's a widow."

Jarvis blinked, then barked out a laugh. "Don't get any ideas."

Lauren shrugged with an innocent expression plastered on her face. "I wouldn't dream of it."

For as long as she'd known the detective, he'd been alone. She knew he'd been married once and had grown kids whom he didn't see often. It hurt her heart to think of him lonely. Loneliness was such a horrible way to live. She hadn't realized how lonely she'd been until Sean brightened her world.

The kitchen door opened and Sean walked in, laden down with painting supplies and several large canvasses. He leaned the unfinished oils against the wall and transferred the rest of his burden to the counter.

Lauren made the introduction. "Detective Jarvis, this is Sean Matthews."

The two shook hands. "Glad to meet you, Mr. Matthews."

"Likewise, Detective. And please, call me Sean."

"What's all this?" Jarvis looked at Lauren with curiosity and concern in his sharp blue eyes.

"She's going to paint again," Sean answered, his tone firm.

Jarvis raised his eyebrows. Lauren bit her lip. The detective knew of her fear, knew that she hadn't touched a brush since the Nightmare. He'd been the one to arrange for her to see a therapist specializing in trauma victims. The therapy had been good in some ways but hadn't touched her fear of painting again. The gaping void was still in her life.

"I'm going to try," she said.

Jarvis's expression softened. "Good for you, Lauren." He slid a glance at Sean. "It definitely was divine providence that brought you two together. With your experience, you're the perfect one to help her."

Sean paled.

"What do you mean?" Lauren asked, feeling like she was missing something.

Jarvis looked at her speculatively. "I did a background check on Sean before leaving L.A. He's a guidance counselor at a Christian high school. Or at least he was until he quit six months ago. You didn't know?"

Surprise vacuumed the air from her lungs as she shook her head. What happened six months ago? Her gaze sought Sean's. His midnight-blue eyes were guarded as he stared at her. That explained why he was outside her door all night and why he was so eager to help her paint.

She was just another "case study" for him.

Sean could see the questions in Lauren's eyes. It pained him to think he'd lost some of her trust by hiding his past from her. As he laid down plastic tarps to protect the carpet, his gut clenched. He'd been trying so hard to avoid this moment. And here it was. Of course the detective would have run a background check on him. Sean should have anticipated having to reveal sooner rather than later his past failure. Shame bore down on him like a mallet hitting its mark. He didn't want Lauren thinking badly of him. He wasn't sure when her opinion of him had become so important to him. But it had.

Thankfully, the detective had departed for the local police station with the promise to return later, while Aunt Mary had gone to the grocery store. Now Sean and Lauren were alone. The air was charged with nervous energy. His and hers.

Lauren glanced warily at the makeshift art studio he'd constructed. She opened the drapes, which let in some natural light. She moved to settle on a dining chair with her back to the window and stared at a large, unfinished landscape on an easel that he'd brought from her house. This picture was of the quaint California town of Carmel-by-the-Sea. He recognized the Carmel mission in the background. One half of the canvas showed the variations in the color of buildings and sidewalks, flowers appeared to dance in sunlight. The other half of the canvas had the penciled etchings that completed the picture.

She was so talented. He wanted to help her reclaim her gift. The way she bit her lip as she contemplated the easel revealed so much vulnerability and made him want to take her in his arms and hold her close. "Lauren," he prompted.

The deep red sweats she wore today showed off her pale skin, shiny, raven-hued hair and warm, toffee-colored eyes.

Attraction flared white hot. He forced himself to take a deep, slow breath as he regained control of his pulse.

"What happened six months ago?" she asked.

Resigned to the deal he'd have to make, he held out a brush. "I'll tell you while you paint."

Her mouth quirked. "A bribe. Is that a counseling technique?"

"Today it is."

She took the brush, ran her fingers over the bristles in a wistful caress. A yearning to have her touch him so gently, so lovingly arched through him.

Moving to the table, she picked up a tube of paint, opened the cap and squeezed pigment onto a plastic palette. Her hands stilled. She sucked in a breath.

Concern lanced his heart. He moved to her side, ready to offer whatever she needed.

"I haven't smelled paint since that night."

"Smell is very evocative," he stated quietly, resisting the urge to reach for her. "Think of a time before that night. A time when you were happy painting."

She closed her eyes. "The day my father gave me my first set of paints."

A soft smile touched her lips, drawing Sean's focus. He longed to taste her lips, to feel the soft tenderness of her mouth beneath his. He forced himself to step back as she opened her eyes.

"Your turn," she said.

He ran a hand through his hair. A knot formed in his chest. Best to just get this over with. "I *was* a high school guidance counselor. Six months ago…a teen boy I was working with committed suicide."

A small gasp escaped from Lauren. She faced him fully, her expression so compassionate he had to look away.

"How awful. How devastating for everyone."

"It was." His heart hurt to remember John's distraught parents. Their anger and accusations. They'd blamed him. And they'd had every right to.

"But why did you quit? Surely, the school needed you more than ever."

"It was my fault," he stated, his voice hoarse with guilt and self-loathing churning inside him.

Lauren set the brush down and moved closer. "Your fault? How so?"

Looking into her intelligent, warm eyes, he could only answer honestly. "I was arrogant enough to think I'd helped him after only a few sessions. I told his parents he was going through typical adolescent angst. I should have seen the signs. I should have paid more attention."

"What signs could you have seen? Did the boy talk about suicide with you?"

Agitation pulsed in his veins. "No. And that's just it." Guilt punched him in the gut. "If I'd been really listening, I would have picked up on the subtext."

"Was there subtext?"

"I—I don't know." He'd gone over every conversation he'd had with John, looking for the clues he'd missed, but they still eluded him. Frustration ate away at his confidence. Regret demolished what was left. "There had to have been. And I just didn't clue into them." The knot in his chest tightened, constricting his breath.

"What was it you told me the other night? About free will?" She put her hand on his clenched fist. "This kid had free will. Whatever his problems were, he chose suicide rather than facing them. You can't blame yourself for something that was out of your control."

Having his words turned back on himself stung and yet… His pulse picked up speed with something that almost felt like hope. Was she right?. But he refused to give ground to the words ricocheting through his heart. She didn't understand. He couldn't forgive himself.

He released his fist and turned his hand so that their palms were pressed together. "I don't deserve your empathy."

A sad light entered her eyes. "Of course you do. You're a good man, Sean. With a good heart. This wasn't your fault."

He wished he could believe her rationale. He hated the guilt, hated feeling so bad. Hated even more knowing how much he'd disappointed God.

But he'd been given a second chance to help someone.

With his free hand, he reached around her to pick up the brush. "Start with one small stroke. You can do it."

Swallowing hard, she fixed her gaze on the brush. "I'm not ready for this."

"Sure you are." He put the brush in her hand and turned her around to face the canvas.

For a long moment she stood frozen in place. Then very deliberately, she dipped the brush into the gooey paint until the bristles were liberally covered in a color like a summer day. Tears welled in her eyes. With a barely audible groan, she flung the paint against the canvas. Blue splattered over the half-finished work.

A sob caught in her throat. "I've ruined it."

"No. You've painted." Heart pounding, he quickly uncapped another tube and squeezed yellow paint onto the palette. She needed to do this in order to unlock the mental block preventing her from moving forward. He could see it so clearly. "Here."

With a soft keening sound, she dipped the brush in the yellow, combining the paints in streaks. With a louder cry, she flung the mixture at the canvas again, adding more splattered texture.

As fast as he could, Sean added more colors to the palette. Sobbing openly now, Lauren splattered color after color over the canvas at a feverish pitch until there was nothing of the original design left.

Abruptly, she dropped the brush, buried her face in her hands and wept.

Moved to tears himself, Sean engulfed her in an embrace. "It's beautiful."

She shook her head against his chest.

He eased her back and took her face in his hands. "It's art."

She took a shuddering breath. "It's not good art."

The constriction around his chest eased a bit. He brushed a paint-streaked tear from her cheek. "I'm sure we can find someone in New York or Los Angeles to buy it."

She made a noise he could claim was a laugh.

"But you painted. Adrian hasn't won."

She blinked as his words seemed to register. Before she could refute his statement, he dipped his head and captured her lips, wanting somehow to convey her worth, her beauty in a tangible way. His heart expanded in his chest as she accepted his kiss, returning it with a sweetness that almost brought tears to his eyes. Deep inside, he knew the moment went beyond attraction to a level that both scared and thrilled him.

Slowly, he eased his lips away and rested his forehead against hers.

When his breathing resumed a more normal rhythm, he removed the paint-splattered canvas and replaced it with the unfinished seascape that had taken his breath away when he'd seen it the first night they'd met. He brought out a fresh brush and palette and unopened tubes of paint. He put the handle of the brush in her hand and then closed his hand around hers. "We'll do it together. Slow and steady."

With heartbreaking vulnerability reflected in the depths of her dark eyes, she nodded. He turned her toward the painting and moved in close behind her. Awareness of her threatened to destroy his good intentions. He forced himself to stay focused on helping her by guiding her hand, first to the paint and then to the canvas. For a moment, the brush hovered there. He waited, his breath held tight in his lungs. Finally, under her own power, the brush began to move in small, brief strokes. Sean slowly removed his hand from hers as triumph flooded his veins. She was painting again. On her own.

She didn't need him anymore.

Now, why did the thought fill him with such emptiness?

Adrian watched the monitor on the laptop from the shadowed confines of the white utility van. The LCD screen showed a clear view of Lauren through the open curtain of the bed-and-breakfast's dining room, even with the drizzling rain splattering the small camera he'd attached to the telephone pole.

She was painting again.

Just like she'd been that night when he'd walked by the art gallery. He'd caught a glimpse of her porcelain skin and shiny black hair and had needed to know what she felt like, smelled like. He'd waited all day for her employees to leave. He'd expected to follow her home but she'd stayed. So he'd found a way inside the gallery. Oh, she'd been a feisty one. He'd been thrilled by the challenge until her candle and solvent burst into flames and burned him. Until she'd ruined him.

Rage clogged his veins. He'd been so close today to making his move, he could have sworn the smell of revenge crackled in the air. But then that detective, the one from his trial, showed up. Hate boiled in Adrian's blood.

Detective Jarvis had been relentless in his questions, but Adrian had never confessed anything. They'd got him dead to rights with Lauren, but not the others—the four they knew about and the dozen they didn't.

He grinned to himself. He was so clever. His mama would be proud—if she'd lived. But she'd been the first to go. The first to realize his power.

Lauren was proving to be by far his most challenging conquest. But he'd persevere and show her she couldn't make a fool of him. His mama hadn't raised a wimp. No, sirree. He could almost hear his mother's cackle as she brought the thin switch down on his back. No wimps allowed. Didn't matter that he couldn't help being scrawny and bug-eyed.

No woman wanted a wimp. And if he let Lauren think she'd won, his mama would be proved right. That was something he couldn't allow. Lauren would have to pay for ruining his life and for making him feel like the wimp his mama had accused him of being. Oh, yes, Lauren would pay.

Tonight, he'd show Lauren just how strong, how patient, how much...*more* he was than she could even fathom.

SEVEN

The shrill sound of a siren tore Lauren from her dreams. She bolted upright, heart pounding, and clutched the covers to her chest. For a disoriented moment, she struggled to make sense of the world around her.

She'd gone to bed keyed up with her successful return to painting, and the amazing kiss that had shifted her world. It had been so long since she'd felt the intimacy of a kiss. She forced herself not to read too much into the gesture. He'd been moved by her painting, by the healing taking place. Nothing more. Right?

Still, thanks to Sean's insistent push and attentive support, she'd been able to paint again. She'd managed to finish a piece, which she planned to give to Mary for Christmas. The feat was so cathartic—cleaning out that place in her that Adrian had tainted. Accomplishing something she'd been afraid to attempt for so long bolstered her confidence and felt good. So had having Sean's arms around her, holding her as she sobbed into his chest. Did all of his "cases" break down like that?

He needed to go back to his calling of helping people. He was really good at it. She hurt to think he blamed himself for the teenager's death. A burden Sean shouldn't have to carry. A burden she wanted to help him lift, as he had done for her.

The jarring intensity of the siren grew louder and closer.

Something was wrong.

She slipped from the bed and hurried to the door. As she exited, Detective Jarvis charged out of his room, wearing plaid drawstring pants, a T-shirt and no shoes. He clutched his sidearm in his hands.

"Get back inside your room until I know what this is about," he ordered and ran down the hall, nearly colliding with Sean as he hit the bottom stair. "Keep an eye on her," Jarvis barked before flinging open the front door and barreling out.

Flashing lights of emergency vehicles penetrated the curtains on the front side of the bed-and-breakfast. Lauren sucked in a sharp breath, fighting flashbacks to her nightmare.

The door next to her burst open. Lauren let out a startled squawk.

"There's a fire at the neighbors'," Mary said, as she hustled out of her room. She secured the sash on her pale yellow robe.

Fire. A horrified shudder ripped through Lauren.

Sean took Mary by the elbow and led her toward Lauren's room. "You two stay in here. I'll be right back." He rushed out, shutting the door behind him.

Feeling trapped and helpless, Lauren tried to keep calm for Mary's sake, even though she wanted to run as far as she could in the direction opposite the fire. But fear kept her frozen in place.

There was one thing she could do. She could pray. The need to reach out to God filled her soul.

"Mary, will you pray with me?" she asked, uncertain that her own prayers would be heard.

"Of course," Mary responded and took her hands.

With hesitation, Lauren began to speak and, as words of faith rolled off her tongue, her voice grew stronger, more vibrant. A sense of wholeness expanded in Lauren's chest, pushing out all the old anger and blame. Her pleas for God's protection, her declaration of love for Him filled the room and then slowly quieted to a hushed reverence as she finished with *Amen*.

Tears misted Mary's eyes. She squeezed Lauren's hands. "Thank you, dear. That was lovely."

Taking a cleansing breath, Lauren felt God's love in her soul.

Several minutes later, Sean opened the door. "The fire department has the fire under control. The family got out unscathed."

Relieved by the news, Lauren asked, "Do they have any idea how it started?"

"I don't know. Maybe Jarvis will have more answers," Sean replied.

"Well, we won't be getting any more sleep tonight," Mary stated briskly. "I'll put on a pot of coffee." She moved out of the room. Lauren and Sean followed. "Sean, invite the Krinkles in," Mary suggested. "We'll make room for them here. We can't have them spending Christmas in some generic hotel."

"That's generous of you, Aunt Mary. I'll go extend the invitation," Sean said and headed back outside.

"What can I do to help?" Lauren asked, hoping Mary's gift for hospitality would rub off on her.

"There are some blankets in the front closet," Mary said. "We should get those out and ready."

As Mary headed for the kitchen, Lauren hobbled toward the front of the house. She shivered as a cold draft hit her exposed skin. She flipped on the light next to the closet, found the blankets and turned with her arms full when her gaze landed on the canvas and easel still set up in the formal dining room.

The blankets fell from her arms as horror iced her veins.

Deep slashes cut the seascape painting to ribbons.

Sean sucked in a sharp breath as he viewed the destruction of Lauren's work. "How did this happen? How could Posar have gotten in?"

"He jimmied open the dining room window." Jarvis slammed his fist on the dining table. "The man's a viper and moves just as sneakily. He most likely set the fire next door as a diversion so he could get in here while we had our guard down."

"But why do this? Why not come after me?" Lauren asked. She leaned against the wall as if she needed the support. Her brown eyes stood out in her pale face.

"Because he's a coward," Jarvis said. "He's just playing with us now. Trying to unnerve us."

"Well, he's certainly doing a bang-up job," Lauren remarked dryly, but with a fragility Sean doubted anyone else noticed.

He moved to her side. "You should sit."

She took his hand. "What I need to do is leave. This was close. The poor Krinkles. What if he decides to attack Mary next? I can't stay here any longer. I need to go away. Find a new hiding place."

Jarvis nodded. "I can get you to a safe house."

Sean's heart twisted in his chest. "But what if he finds her there? What then? You keep moving her?"

"If need be," Jarvis answered, though Sean could see he wasn't happy with the idea.

Squeezing Lauren's hand, Sean's heart twisted. "That's no way to live."

"I know," she said. "I hate that my life has come down to this. But what choice do I have?"

Sean didn't have an answer. He only knew he didn't want her to leave. But the alternative did put her and his aunt in danger. "There has to be a solution."

He'd come to respect and care for Lauren in so many ways. Her courageous, generous spirit brought light to the dark places in his heart. He wanted to protect her, yes, but more than that, he wanted to have her near him always. Wanted to be needed by her for more than just a barrier between her and evil. Selfishly, he longed to have her see him as a man worthy of loving.

But sadly, he knew he didn't deserve her love. He turned to the detective. "Can you get more protection here?"

"Already done."

"So then I become a prisoner here until Posar messes up or loses interest?" Lauren said. "No, thank you. There has to be a way to flush Adrian out when and where we're ready for him."

"We are not using you as bait," Jarvis said, his tone hard.

"But that's exactly what we need to do," she said, excitement vibrating in her voice.

Dread slithered down Sean's spine. "Lauren, what are you thinking?"

"That we bait him." She implored him with her beautiful eyes. "Set a trap. It's the only way I'll ever get my life back."

"I'm not going to put your life at risk," Jarvis said. "If you don't want to stay here, I'll move you. But I'm not going to allow you to do something so dangerous."

"It's not really a matter of you allowing me," she said, her tone full of determination. "But you can help me. Both of you. I need to take my life back." She met Sean's gaze. "I've learned I'm more capable than I thought I was. And God willing, we'll take down Posar."

Horrified, Sean stared. "It's not a matter of your capabilities. We're talking about using you as bait. No way!"

She stepped to him and took his hands in hers. "I have to take control of my life. As long as I'm hiding, looking over my shoulder, wondering when he's going to strike, he's won."

The truth of her words were like a knife to Sean's chest. And yet, if something happened to her…he didn't think he could survive it.

He'd just have to make sure nothing happened to her.

"The plan is simple, really," Lauren muttered under her breath as she ducked into a toy store to get out of the drizzling rain.

This morning when Jarvis had said those words as he had explained the plan, she'd agreed, but now, not so much.

After spending time hobbling around town, making herself as visible as possible, Lauren would seemingly move back to her cottage. She would wear a wire all the time and have an under-cover police officer shadowing her. Jarvis and several other officers, including a female officer who would pose as Lauren, would hide out in her cottage, so when she arrived there, she could be spirited back to the relative safety of the bed-and-breakfast.

Unfortunately, the wire taped to her chest and attached to a two-by-two square transmitter at her waistband itched, the rain wouldn't let up and Lauren's ankle ached. She hadn't realized how much she'd been babying her foot until she'd spent several hours using only the crutch to support herself on the concrete and wood slated sidewalks of Cannon Beach. Even ducking into stores for some much-needed breaks from the rain and some Christmas shopping did little to alleviate the pain and fatigue, not to mention the stress of knowing that Posar was out there. Hopefully, watching her.

Her colorful sweat suit topped with a bright yellow rain slicker were hard to miss.

So here she was, pretending to be interested in a locally crafted toy when all she wanted to do was lie down in a hot bath and soak away the stress of the past few days. But that wasn't going to happen anytime soon.

With a resigned sigh, she made her way back to the boardwalk, awkwardly clutching the bags of her day's Christmas gift purchases and heading toward the south end of Cannon Beach's main street.

It was late in the afternoon when Sean picked her up in his truck in front of Cannon Beach Playhouse. Once she hit the seat, exhaustion settled in. She leaned back and closed her eyes for the short drive to her cottage.

Sean helped her to the front door. "I'll be waiting for you in the truck."

The arrangement was for Sean to wait on the street behind her house. An officer would escort Lauren out her back door, across both her backyard and the neighbor's and around to the street with Sean's waiting truck. Then he'd whisk her to safety.

With a hand on his arm she stopped Sean from walking away. "Thank you for everything."

"You don't need to thank me. I'm glad to help."

"And you have," she stated. Her gaze caressed his handsome face. "You've helped me in so many ways. You've given me the strength to face my fear of painting again. Helped me find the courage to go through with this plan. But more importantly, you helped me to fully accept God back into my life."

With a gentle hand, he touched her cheek. "I'm glad."

"I just wish you'd take your own advice and let God heal you."

His expression closed and he stepped back. "I'd better go."

A shaft of frustration arced through her. She grabbed his hand. He paused, his gaze questioning.

Emotions welled in her chest. This man had taught her about living life, about seizing back what was lost. He'd taught her to face her fear and to trust God's plan for her life, for her heart. Clarity sharpened her focus to one single thought. She loved him. That both terrified and delighted her.

Tugging him closer, she murmured impulsively, "Kiss me."

His eyes widened, the color deepening to a blue that matched the churning surf.

"Gladly," he said and captured her lips.

The soft pressure ignited a firestorm of yearning through Lauren just as it had before. Only then she'd been so emotionally distraught and so in need. Now, she could truly appreciate the sheer happiness she felt in his arms, for as long as it lasted. She longed to deepen the contact, to linger in the sensations. She could easily romanticize their kisses, make them mean something more. Something real and permanent. Could almost convince herself that he loved her back.

But she didn't. She knew better. There was no future there. Nothing good would come of wishing she could be more than a friend or an obligation to Sean.

She broke the kiss. And felt like she'd just broken a piece of her heart.

Keeping her gaze downcast so he wouldn't see how affected she was by the simple caress, she said, "See you at the truck."

She rushed inside the cottage.

The last of the sun's rays winked out as Adrian slowed the white utility van to a stop at the street corner to watch Lauren climb out of the jogger's truck and hobble toward the front door. Pulling the brim of his navy cap lower, he sliced a glance toward the two cops sitting in the unmarked car on the opposite side of the street. Better play the part, he thought.

He picked up the clipboard from the passenger seat and pretended to write as if he were nothing more than what he seemed, a common Joe doing his job. His gaze slid back to Lauren.

His blood boiled. She allowed that man to kiss her.

She'd pay for that.

The quick rap of knuckles on the driver's side window jerked his breath out of his lungs. Slowly, so as not to reveal how frantically his heart was beating, he turned his head just enough so he could see who was there. One of the plainclothes officers stood beside the van, his badge visible. He was older, with graying hair and a trim physique.

Adrian rolled the window down. "Problem, Officer?"

"What are you doing here?" Sharp gray eyes assessed him.

Keeping the scarred side of his face turned away from the window, Adrian said, "Had a report there was a downed telephone line on this street, but I don't see it. Do you?"

"No downed lines. Move along."

The jogger left Lauren to enter her home, drove his truck to the intersection and turned. She was alone. The timing couldn't have been better.

"Yes, sir." Adrian started the van.

The officer stepped back as Adrian pressed on the gas and eased the van away from the curb. He slowly drove down the street, keeping a good distance from the black truck as he followed it around the block to make sure the jogger was really leaving. When the truck doubled back and turned down the street that ran parallel to the back of Lauren's house, Adrian rolled past. The truck stopped in front of the house whose backyard adjoined Lauren's backyard.

Adrian barked out a laugh as he pressed on the gas and drove away.

They thought they were so smart. Ha! He'd show them. He'd show them all just how clever *he* was.

Lauren entered the dimly lit cottage and tried to catch her breath. What had she been thinking, asking Sean to kiss her again?

A moment of insanity, for sure, because as soon as it was done, she became more acutely aware of how much she loved him and how hard it would be when they parted. What she felt for Sean was deeper, more mature than anything she'd ever felt before. And the loss would be that much greater.

She shook off the disturbing thoughts brought on by the kiss and focused on Detective Jarvis, who was introducing her to the other officers in her living room.

"Officer Garrett will escort you back to the bed-and-breakfast and stay there with you," Jarvis explained.

Lauren extended her hand to the officer. He was tall, with wide shoulders and a chiseled jaw. She estimated he was in his late thirties, possibly early forties. "Thank you."

"Not a problem," he said in a deep tone.

"You met our decoy, Officer Rachel Sims, earlier." Jarvis gestured toward the pretty, dark-haired woman who rose from the couch and glided forward.

There was a resemblance, Lauren thought. Rachel was the same height as Lauren, had a similar pale complexion and wide-set dark eyes. Lauren found it disturbing to see another woman wearing her favorite sweats outfit. "Officer Sims, I appreciate you taking this risk."

She inclined her head. "It's my job."

Lauren turned to Jarvis. "Should she have the wire now?"

"She has her own." Jarvis reached to Lauren's side and fiddled with the transmitter, then took her elbow and guided her toward the back door. "Come on, let's get you out of here."

Officer Garrett went through the door first then motioned for Lauren to join him on the porch. She stepped out and then, as hurriedly as her twisted ankle would allow, followed the officer down the stairs, across the small expanse of lawn to the back fence.

"You'll have to squeeze through," he said as he pried several wooden slats away from the rails.

Biting her lip, she asked, "What will the neighbors think?"

"They've been sent out to dinner, compliments of the Cannon Beach Police Department."

"Nice, but you're destroying the fence slats."

He waved away her concern. "They can easily be nailed back on."

Ducking beneath the middle rail, she squeezed through the opening. The Ace bandage wrapped around her foot snagged on the bottom rail and she tripped, going down on her hands and knees.

Tennis shoes appeared in her line of vision and hands reached for her.

She sucked in a breath as Sean helped her to stand. In the waning light of the day, his handsome face showed concern.

"You okay?" he asked.

"Just clumsy," she replied, feeling heat creep up her neck.

"We should get moving," Officer Garrett prompted.

Sean looped his arm around Lauren's waist and half carried her across the neighbors' mushy lawn toward the gate that led to the street. Sean's truck stood at the curb. The three of them piled into the cab with Lauren in the middle as Sean drove to the bed-and-breakfast. When he pulled the truck to a stop, Lauren's gaze was drawn to the white utility van on the corner. It looked just like the one that had shown up the other day. She glanced at the dashboard clock. It was after five. The workday had ended.

She touched Sean's hand before he climbed out of the truck. "Seems a little late in the day for the repair guy to be working, don't you think?"

Officer Garrett opened the passenger door. "You two stay put. I'll go check it out." He climbed out, shutting the door behind him.

With his hand on his gun, the officer approached the van from the driver's side. He peered through the window. Apparently there was no one in the front seat. He rounded the front end and disappeared from view.

The passenger side door of Sean's truck jerked open. Lauren let out a startled yelp as someone slid onto the seat next to her. Something hard pressed into her ribs. She froze.

"Drive, or I shoot her now," a familiar, deep voice barked.

Lauren gaped at the man dressed in blue coveralls with a navy cap pulled low over his dark, menacing eyes.

Adrian.

The world tilted as the blood drained from Lauren's brain. He hadn't taken the bait. And now they were at his mercy.

EIGHT

Heart pounding with fear for Lauren, Sean started the truck and pressed on the gas. "Where are we going?"

"Head to Highway 101 and go south," Posar said, leaning forward to stare at Sean as he removed his hat and peeled away a fake beard.

Sean tried to stifle his reaction to the horrible scars marring the right side of Posar's face. The twisted and puckered skin made his eye bulge in a grotesque way. His ear, now visible without the cap, was nothing more than a hole in his head.

The muffled shouts of Officer Garrett drew Sean's gaze to the rearview mirror. The officer was running after them. Gripping the steering wheel tight, Sean said, "You'll never get away with this."

The man chuckled, a sinister sound that reverberated through the cab of the truck. "We'll see."

Sean glanced at Lauren. She appeared to be in

shock. Her face had gone pasty white, her breathing shallow as she stared straight ahead.

Posar slid his arm around Lauren, his gloved hand clamping on her shoulder. "Miss me?" Posar said. She whimpered and leaned toward Sean.

Anger mushroomed in Sean's veins. "Leave her alone."

Keeping his hold on her, Posar waved a nasty-looking gun at him. "You mind yourself there, jogger man. I'm the one with the gun and I'll do as I please."

Their lives were in the hands of a madman. A shudder of dread coursed through Sean. Only God could protect them. He sent up a silent plea for God's protection, because Sean couldn't protect them any more than he could have saved the boy in his counsel. There was nothing he could do.

No, wait. He dropped one hand from the steering wheel and put his fingers to Lauren's side and felt for the wire, following it until he reached the small battery transmitter-box taped at her waistband. Yes! It was still there.

Sean chanced a risky glance to his hand where it exposed the little black box. Shouldn't there be a light indicating it was active?

He met Lauren's frantic gaze.

"Two hands on the wheel, jogger man. Safer that way," Adrian said.

Sean found the power switch and flipped it before replacing his hand on the steering wheel. He hoped he'd just activated the device.

Roughly thirteen excruciating miles later, a parking lot just off the highway became visible in the glow of the truck's headlights. No cars were present.

"This is good," Posar said to Sean. "Pull over."

"Cape Falcon. Why here?"

"Because I said so."

Sean did as commanded, praying the wire would still transmit even though they were far from Cannon Beach. But in case it didn't, his mind ran through possible plans of escape. He was going to have to try to take the gun from Posar. That would be the only way to get Lauren out of this. He brought the truck to a halt. Posar slid out the passenger door and yanked Lauren out with him.

Still holding the gun on her, he said, "You, too."

Sean climbed from the truck and rounded the front.

"Start walking." Posar gestured with the gun toward a trailhead barely discernible among the giant spruce trees and salal plants covering the forested ground.

"We can't negotiate the trail to the cliffs in the dark," Sean said, hoping Jarvis heard.

"Doesn't make much difference to me if I kill you now or later." When Sean didn't move, Posar aimed the gun at his chest. "Your decision."

Sean met Lauren's terrified gaze. He had to stay alive long enough to help Lauren escape. He wasn't going to let this monster kill the woman he loved.

He sucked in a quick breath. He did love her. And would willingly die trying to save her. Failure was not an option.

"Fine. We'll head up the trail." Sean turned and set out in the dark.

Posar pushed Lauren ahead of him. She stumbled as her bum foot hit an uneven patch in the crude hiking trail. His hand bit into her arm as he steadied her.

"Walk," he barked.

"I'm trying, but I can't see where to step," she replied through gritted teeth.

Pain shot up her leg. Fear beat against her temples. They'd been hiking for a while along a forested ridge. The sounds of the highway had long faded to be replaced with the noises of small birds and nocturnal animals foraging for food in the underbrush. The temperature had dropped significantly, making her limbs stiff with cold. Damp, salt-scented wind added to the chill. The roar of the crashing ocean grew louder.

Up ahead, she could see Sean's silhouette, a dark shadow in the inky night. He kept glancing back. Though she doubted he could see her face clearly, she tried to be brave for him but tears of terror and pain still slipped from her eyes. She prayed to God to keep him safe.

"Veer to your right," Adrian called out.

Sean headed in that direction. She and Adrian followed.

They came out of the forest into a clearing. The moon's light revealed the sharply distinct edge of a cliff.

Sean stopped and turned to face them.

Adrian pushed Lauren toward Sean. Startled, she cried out as she fell, coming down hard on her already bruised knees. Pain exploded when nerve endings sizzled at the impact.

Sean moved swiftly to her side.

"Stop!" Adrian shouted.

Without acknowledging him, Sean squatted beside her. In a low whisper, he said, "Follow my lead." Louder, he asked, "Can you stand?"

Anxious yet encouraged that he had something planned, she nodded. "Yes."

With his help, she managed to get back on her feet.

With his arm around her waist, Sean faced Adrian. "What now? You shoot us?"

At Sean's gentle nudge, she slowly moved away from the cliff.

"Oh, no. That would be too easy, too quick," Adrian gloated. "Step away from her."

"No. You want her, you'll either have to shoot me or come through me to get her," Sean said, his voice hard and determined.

Lauren swallowed back the bile that rose as alarm bubbled in her gut. They were slowly inching their way farther from the edge.

Adrian moved closer. "Don't you think I'm tempted to just shoot you and be done with it? You've caused me enough trouble already. If it weren't for you, I'd have had her days ago!"

Continuing to inch their way back toward the forest, Lauren taunted, "You're a monster who deserves to be locked up for the rest of your life."

Adrian sneered. "Prison walls can't keep me. I'll just burn them down again. And again. And again.

And again." His deep, guttural laughter revealed more about his insanity than his words.

"Detective Jarvis will hunt you down," she said.

"Not if I get him first," Adrian stated. Now his back faced the cliffs. "Stop moving. I know what you're trying to do but you won't get away. I'll drop you both before you take two steps."

Sean gave her side a quick squeeze before removing his arm from around her. She didn't know what he planned to do. She wanted to grab his hand and keep him from trying anything foolish. But he stepped away from her.

"You're nothing but a coward," Sean taunted as he moved farther away from Lauren. "Put the gun down and let's see who drops who."

"Good try, but I don't think so. My mama didn't raise a fool. I know I couldn't beat you in a fist fight, but I'm smarter than you are, pretty boy. And I have the advantage." He raised the gun.

"No!" Lauren shouted.

"Run!" Sean commanded.

Adrian swung the gun in her direction.

She froze. Sean launched himself at Adrian, knocking him back. They grappled for the gun. Sean was bigger and stronger, but Adrian had a wildness that could have only been fueled by madness. Sean drove Adrian toward the cliff's edge as they struggled for control over the weapon. Lauren's heart slammed against her chest in painful beats.

"Oh, please, dear Jesus, protect Sean."

The sharp, loud retort of the gun firing echoed inside Lauren's head. She watched in horror as blood spread across Sean's shoulder, and yet he didn't give up struggling to push Adrian toward the edge.

Adrian slammed his fist into Sean's wound. Sean grunted and seemed to deflate slightly. The momentum of the fight turned and Adrian began to push Sean toward the cliff. Fear and love for Sean galvanized Lauren into action. She couldn't just stand there while Adrian killed the man she loved. She ran as fast as her injured foot would allow and collided with Adrian. Caught by surprise, he staggered back, precariously close to the cliff's edge, his feet slipping on loosened earth and rocks. The gun he'd wrenched control of swung toward her.

With a primal growl, Sean rammed his shoulder into Adrian's gut, sending him stumbling sideways. Adrian cursed and attempted to turn toward Scan, but lost his footing on the uneven ground. Arms flailing, he tried to regain his balance, but couldn't.

Lauren watched in shock as he went tumbling over the cliff's edge. His scream echoed through the inky night—and then all was silent.

For a long moment, Lauren stared at the spot where Adrian had been. Then her gaze fell on Sean, who'd fallen to his knees. She dropped to his side. "You're going to be okay," she said, her voice breaking with a sob.

"I did it," he said in a weak voice. "I saved you."

"Yes. Yes, you did."

Sean smiled before slumping over. He'd passed out. Frantic, Lauren shook him. "Wake up. Wake up."

How was she going to get him out of here?

A crashing sound coming from the forest sent new fear sliding through her. Would she now have to contend with some other sort of monstrous beast?

Then Jarvis and several other officers charged into the clearing, flashlights blazing and guns drawn. Blinking, barely believing what she was seeing, Lauren said, "How…? How can you be here?"

Jarvis knelt beside her. "The wire. We heard everything once it was switched back on. Plus, it has a tracking device."

In all the chaos of the last few hours, she'd forgotten. She clutched his arm. "Sean's been shot. We need to get him to the hospital."

"I know." He took her elbow and pulled her away from him. "Let the EMTs take care of him."

Lauren nodded as two uniformed emergency personnel moved in to tend to Sean. They bandaged his wound and lifted him onto a litter before carrying him out of the clearing.

"Where's Posar?" Jarvis asked.

She looked to the cliff. "He's gone."

Jarvis left her side to peer over the edge of the cliff. When he returned, he put his arm around her and steered her toward the trail. "Let's get out of here."

Sean lay in the hospital bed, staring at the porous, stuccoed ceiling. He could make out the faint strands of a Christmas carol playing on a radio somewhere outside the room.

His shoulder was on fire again but he didn't want to ask for more pain medication because it made him loopy and sleepy. Aunt Mary had said Lauren had kept a vigil while he was in surgery to remove the bullet lodged in his shoulder and was now waiting to come in. He wanted, no *needed*, to be fully awake and coherent when she arrived.

Now that the threat to her life was gone, was

she preparing to return to California? She'd once said there were too many memories there, but was that still true? If she didn't leave, would she stay in Cannon Beach? Were there too many memories here as well?

Was she coming to say goodbye?

Anguish seared his heart.

He didn't want her to leave. He wanted her to stay. With him.

Was the need to confess his feelings selfish? Would it be better to hold back? Didn't she deserve the truth?

Did he deserve to have a chance with her?

He was afraid the answer to that question was no. He didn't deserve her. He didn't deserve happiness.

His eyes slid closed as tears threatened to escape.

A whisper of movement alerted him that he was no longer alone. He opened his eyes and focused on Lauren's beautiful face. She smiled, her dark eyes lighting up.

"I didn't mean to disturb you, but I'm glad you're awake," she said in a rush. A blush pinkened her cheeks.

"You didn't wake me." He held out his hand on his uninjured side. "I've been waiting for you."

She grasped his hand and held on tight. Her eyes shifted to his bandaged shoulder. "Does it hurt terribly?"

He let out a short laugh. "Yeah. Like crazy."

"I'm sorry. You were so brave." Tears filled her pretty eyes. "This shouldn't have happened to you."

Frustration spiked his pulse. "It wasn't your fault. You have to stop owning Posar's actions."

"But I brought that monster into your life."

She also brought love. And salvaged his relationship with God. He squeezed her hand. "Stop it. I wouldn't change one thing, because otherwise I would never have met you."

She blinked, clearly taken aback. "Really?"

How could she not know how he felt? One of his grandfather's sayings floated through his mind, *In for a penny, in for a pound.* "Yes, really. I love you, Lauren. I can't imagine what my life would be like without you."

"You love me?"

She said it as if she had trouble believing him. He wished he could take her into his arms and kiss her until she believed him. His injury wouldn't allow that, so he lifted her hand to his lips and pressed a kiss to her knuckles. The long sleeve of her bright green sweatshirt rode up, giving a peak of the grafted skin beneath. "I do. But I know I don't deserve you. I don't deserve such happiness."

With her free hand, she tugged the sleeve down. "No. It's me who doesn't deserve you. I'm so ugly. My scars are so ugly."

The vulnerability in her expression tore at his heart. He touched a finger to her lips "I don't ever want to hear you say that again. You are beautiful. Inside and outside. And I'm humbled by your bravery of overcoming your past."

Joy exploded in her expression. "I love you, too. I don't want to live my life without you, either." Her eyebrows drew together as her expression dimmed. "Only…" Her teeth tugged on her bottom lip. "You taught me the only way to healing is to face my fears. I think the same can be said of you. We can't be together until you've come to terms with your past. I know you have the strength to. With God's help, you can do anything."

The air left his lungs in a rush. Face his past. Face the fact that he couldn't help a boy who didn't want to be helped.

Grace.

His heart hammered as the word echoed through his mind. For a moment he fought to hold on to the guilt, but with Lauren clutching his hand and God knocking at the door to his heart, his mind and soul, he finally let go and felt the inpouring of love, joy and peace of God, filling him to overflowing. It wasn't a complete healing. It would take time to overcome all his guilt and grief. But it was a start.

Feeling lighter than he had in six long months, he said, "You're right, Lauren. So very right."

A smile played at the corners of her mouth. "I am."

"But I can't do it alone. I'll need you by my side."

"Just try to get rid of me," she teased.

He pulled her closer until her lips were inches from his. "What a wonderful Christmas present God has given me this year," he murmured.

"He's given this gift to us both," she replied before closing the gap between them.

* * * * *

Dear Reader,

The setting for this novella, Cannon Beach, Oregon, is one of my favorite places. The quaint town and beautiful beaches, whether in summer or winter, draw crowds of Oregonians as well as tourists from all across the world. The idea for this story came to me many years ago while vacationing here. As I sat on the warm sand one summer day, with the surf as background music and the majesty of Haystack Rock looming out of the water, I closed my eyes and let my mind go. I saw Sean running down the deserted beach on a cold, winter's evening. I heard Lauren's cry for help. And from there the story morphed into what you've read.

I hope you found Lauren and Sean a compelling couple with problems that seemed insurmountable but, as we know, with God anything is possible. Even overcoming a madman bent on revenge. But most importantly, finding healing and love through faith.

Until we meet again, may God's loving hand be upon you.

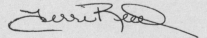

QUESTIONS FOR DISCUSSION

1. In what ways were Sean and Lauren realistic characters? How did their romance build believably?

2. Sean felt guilt for the suicide death of the boy he was counseling. Was the death something Sean could control? Have you ever had someone close to you commit suicide? How did you handle their death?

3. What did you think of the villain, Adrian Posar? Do you feel, as Lauren did, that God shouldn't allow men like him to have free will? What would human life be like if there was no free will?

4. Lauren was angry and questioned why God allowed her to be hurt. Can you tell of a time when you felt this way? How did you come to terms with the feeling?

5. Lauren felt that her scars made her ugly. Is outward appearance the only way we can feel ugly? Do you have scars, either physical

or emotional, that make you feel ugly? How can we overcome this feeling?

6. Sean and his aunt opened their home to a stranger in need. Was there a time when you were given an opportunity to open your home to someone in need? And if you invited them in, tell how the experience affected you. If you didn't invite them in, tell why not.

7. Did you notice the Scripture in the beginning of the story? What application does it have to your life? What are the differences between a heart of stone and a heart of flesh? Why would God want to do this?

CHRISTMAS TARGET
Stephanie Newton

For Sarah Kate and Maggie. You know why.

Acknowledgments

Many, many thanks—

To my editor, Melissa Endlich,
and to Assistant Editor Elizabeth Mazer.
Steeple Hill is blessed with an amazing
editorial staff!

To Brian Stampfl, CSI detective in
Seattle, Washington—for answering questions
and being generally brilliant.

To meteorologist Jason Kelley, for expert advice
(and expert forecasting, of course!).

One of the best parts of writing is learning
new stuff—I love hearing advice and opinions from
the experts about things as I'm writing. Any details
that I get right are usually because of them. Any
details that are wrong are definitely all on me.

Yet I still dare to hope
when I remember this:
The faithful love of the LORD never ends!
His mercies never cease.
—*Lamentations* 3:21, 22

ONE

An unusual silence fell as CSI Maria Fuentes strode into the precinct room. The norm would be everyone grabbing for evidence reports, drilling her with questions, pushing her to finish with their Very Important Evidence that exact minute. When the cops all scattered to hide from her, she knew something was up.

Gabe Sloan peered over the top of his laptop, his brown eyes wide but filled with the kind of mischief that she knew couldn't be good. When it came to finding trouble, criminals had nothing on cops with time on their hands.

She narrowed her eyes and pinned him with her meanest look. "What's going on, cowboy?"

In answer, he picked up the remote control from his desk and unmuted the television. She turned toward it as Ben Storm's handsome face filled the screen. As a scientist, she could understand the appeal of "everyone's favorite weatherman."

The black hair that fell over his eyes just right and the gray eyes that held a promise of something a little dangerous.

But she'd gone to high school with him. She knew better than anyone that the nice-guy routine was just that. A routine.

Her mouth fell open as a picture of herself appeared in the right-hand corner of the screen. Possibly the most unflattering picture ever taken, as she'd bent over evidence, her hair caught up in a knot with a pencil, serviceable black eyeglasses on her face.

Ben Storm laughed as the anchor slapped him on the back. "Congratulations, Ben. I'm sure she's a great girl."

Maria snatched the remote out of Gabe's hand and muted the television again, this time piercing Joe Sheehan with a quelling look. "Am I going to have to ask?"

Joe shifted uneasily beneath her gaze, his muscles bunching under his Sea Breeze Police Department T-shirt. "It was a win-a-date-with-the-weatherman contest and we just thought, you know…"

"We?" She glanced around the room, back to Gabe.

"All us guys." The mischief in Gabe's eyes had

faded and apparently reality was setting in. Like maybe he was realizing it hadn't been such a good idea to prank her. No kidding. "Come on, Maria, we all know how long it's been since you've had a date."

"What am I supposed to do with...*him?*" She vaguely waved a hand at the television. She couldn't bring herself to look at the image of the man who, as a high school senior, had brought her one of the single most humiliating experiences of her life.

Gabe cleared his throat. "Wednesday to Saturday there's a big weather conference in Destin and you're supposed to be his date to the dinners and stuff. Then Saturday you're both coming back here for Sea Breeze's annual charity Christmas ball."

"No. Way."

Real alarm crossed Gabe's features then. "Sailor's heading up the committee for the ball this year, Maria. The television station promised my wife media coverage, and Ben Storm promised a huge donation."

"He doesn't even live here anymore." A headache grew behind her eyes, but she refused to let them see how much this bothered her.

"His parents do. And since he grew up in Sea Breeze, he has ties to the community. Come on,

Maria. We're raising money for the Children's Hospital."

She didn't move, waited until she saw a tiny bead of sweat appear on Gabe's forehead. She sighed. "When is this thing?"

He pushed away from his desk and gestured to one of the other cops, who plopped an overnight bag in front of her. An overnight bag that looked suspiciously like her own.

She looked around the room, from face to smirking cop face. *"Seriously?"*

Joe Sheehan threw one hard arm around her. "Have a good time, honey. Don't worry about the 'kids.' We'll take care of everything."

"Yeah, that's what I'm afraid of." She closed her eyes, her mind swirling. She didn't want to go on *any* date, least of all with Ben Storm. But now that these goobers had gotten her into this, if she didn't go through with it, she'd be letting down the whole town. Not to mention, she'd look like a bad sport in front of the entire police force.

Maybe she could go to the ball and Ben Storm could go to the conference on his own. That would be a compromise they could all live with. As soon as she saw Ben Storm, she would just explain the situation. Surely he would understand.

When she opened her eyes, the cops standing

around took a visible step back. "Oh, yeah. You losers better be afraid. When I get back, you are in so much trouble."

Meteorologist Ben Storm looked at his watch, narrowing his eyes against the wind kicked up by the rotors of the helicopter. He was waiting on some woman named Maria to arrive at the helipad, a woman who would be his date for the weekend, a woman who was now more than ten minutes late.

A decade in television had broken that habit in him. He paced the perimeter of the pad, glanced at his watch again and sighed. Nerves—something he hadn't felt in years—jangled slightly in his belly. Why in the world had he agreed to do this?

Oh, right. Contract renegotiation. He wanted out. This was his compromise with the network. One big publicity stunt to get ratings up and he could move back to his hometown and be the local weather expert, doing only the occasional special report for Weather 24. Less stress, more time to fish. More time with *family*. His big plan.

He took another look at the watch face then glanced around, feeling slightly exposed out here in the open on the helipad. Maybe it was just nerves. His date—Maria, he reminded himself—actually had the upper hand here. She knew who he was. All he knew about her was her name and that she came from his hometown. His coworkers had picked her for him. And it had obviously been a joke.

Since his wife died two years ago, his coworkers had set him up with a string of women. Correction: *tried* to set him up. His friends at work had different priorities than he did. They went for looks first, substance a distant second. And with Ben's life, he couldn't afford to fall for just a pretty face.

Consequently, from the picture of the woman they'd picked, it was obvious that their choice here was a poke at him for turning down all the gorgeous women they'd sent his way.

Well, he didn't have a choice. He had to make the best of it, had to make it work. Hopefully, he would show his date for the weekend the time of her life. And then he could go on with his.

A horn blared as a car came barreling around the corner, red-and-blue lights on the dash flashing. Finally. Wait—his date was a cop?

The sedan jerked to a stop and she climbed out, corkscrews of light brown hair whirling around her face. Fortunately, she had on cargo pants, a T-shirt and boots, rather than the police officer blues he'd been half expecting.

The guy with her didn't have on a uniform either,

but he did have a weapon, right there on his hip. He opened the trunk and tossed an overnight bag at her. She snagged it out of the air and turned toward Ben.

She was small, Ben could see that now, but walked with purpose. All he could see of her face in the wind were those wild, springy curls and her sunglasses against the midday sun.

He met her just outside the edge of the helipad and took her bag, shouting over the noise of the news chopper. His smile was the product of years of practice. "Hi, I'm Ben. You must be Maria. Come on, we've got kind of a time crunch. The news crew is waiting on us in Destin. If the footage is going to make the broadcast, we've got to hurry."

He pitched her bag over the seat and held a hand out to her. She hesitated, but put her hand in his and he gripped it. He gave her an easy boost, but she didn't need it. With athletic grace, she climbed into the chopper and slid into the far seat.

The whine of the engine powered up even as he climbed in beside her, letting his backpack slide down to rest by his feet. He pulled on headphones and motioned to her to do the same. "Okay, so it's a short hop to Destin. We're going to land on the helipad at the Emerald Island resort. The news crew will be on the ground to meet us there. They'll shoot us as we get off the chopper. We'll stop, say a few words. They'll film us getting into the elevators. Easy, right?"

She muttered something about shooting that he didn't catch. He moved her mike closer to her mouth. "'Scuse me?"

"Nothing. I need to talk to you about something." She slid her sunglasses off and he blinked. Her eyes were brown with flecks of gold and rimmed with the most fantastic eyelashes he'd ever seen. Long and dark, they curled almost to her eyebrows. If he couldn't tell she had no makeup on, he'd swear that they were fake. But there was clearly nothing fake about Maria Fuentes.

Ben blinked again. "We'll have plenty of time to talk once we get there."

"No, Ben, I need to—"

He held up a finger, stopping her. The gleam on the aquamarine water outside the window caught his eye. Crab Island, the hangout where locals brought their boats and anchored, had long been a favorite spot of his. He took a deep breath. He was so close to being home free. To being home.

To the pilot he said, "Fly in close. Let the cameras get a good close-up of the helicopter, then circle back and land."

He glanced at his date. She had a slightly green cast to her face. Maybe not a fan of flying? "We'll be there soon. Don't worry—we'll have plenty of time to chat later."

She sank back against the seat. She didn't really seem too excited about their big weekend. In fact, she didn't act like she wanted to be here at all.

His headphones crackled with the pilot's voice. "Coming around for the first pass."

Ben leaned closer to the window. Yep, there was his crew, down there waiting for him and his date. The pilot banked into a turn and within minutes had effortlessly set the chopper on the resort's helipad.

He pulled off his headphones and, out of the corner of his eye, saw his date, Maria, do the same. She'd covered those beautiful eyes with her ugly sunglasses, so he reached up and slid them off, folding them and putting them in his pocket. "Show off those pretty eyes."

She narrowed them and he grinned. "And don't forget to smile. This will be over before you know it."

"Yes, I'm really thrilled and excited to be here with Ben." Maria had said it, but she didn't mean it. She smiled for the camera anyway. The wind on the roof of the resort parking deck whipped her hair into a tangle of unruly curls.

Ben slid an arm around her and gave the camera thumbs-up. "That's a wrap, guys. Not everyone is used to multiple takes and probing personal questions."

The crew laughed and let them pass. And with that one comment, a grudging sense of gratitude found its way into the nothingness she'd forced herself to feel for Ben Storm after he'd stolen her dream. He was more considerate than she'd expected.

The elevator doors glided open as they approached. Ben pulled a slim folder from his pocket and took out a key card, slid it into a slot and punched the top floor. "We have the penthouse."

"Sounds nice, but Ben—"

"You won't believe the view."

Okay, maybe not so considerate after all. Did he have to keep interrupting? She drew in a breath to start again and instead slanted a glance at him. As they rose, he stared at the numbers. It seemed that he didn't recognize her at all from all those years ago. She shook her head. Did it even matter?

He stepped forward as the doors opened directly into the penthouse living room and held them for her to pass.

She hadn't been prepared, not at all, for what she would see. Every surface gleamed with luxury. Marble floors, sumptuous furnishings, exquisite stone countertops. Without a doubt, no expense had been spared, but beyond the obvious opulence of the suite of rooms, the bank of windows offered an unimpaired view of the Gulf of Mexico.

Almost without conscious thought, she walked toward the window, catching her breath at the color of the water. Aqua fading to emerald, it defied description.

"Breathtaking, isn't it?" She hadn't heard him walk up beside her, but took an instinctive step away from him.

"The gulf almost always is, even at its worst." She remembered that she needed to talk to him. "Ben, I can't stay here."

A grin spread across his face, showing his perfectly even row of gleaming white teeth. Even his teeth were pretty. In comparison, she felt like the ugly duckling.

"You aren't expected to stay with me, if that's what you're worried about. There's an adjoining suite, called a lockout. It has its own entrance and elevator—and a locking door." He walked toward the expansive dining table, a sea of glass topped with a huge arrangement of fruit and chocolates.

"That's not it." She corrected herself. "I mean, that's nice, but here's the thing, Ben. I didn't sign up for this. My coworkers entered me in this contest, sent in that horrible picture and basically set me up. I really can't do this."

His eyes went hard and for a moment—just a split second, really—she saw the boy he'd once been. The tough kid, fighting his way in and out of trouble and then to the top of the class. But just that fast, he was the smooth-talking stranger again. "I'm not sure I follow."

"It was a joke, Ben. They thought it would be funny." She took two steps away from him, dragged a breath into her too-tight chest. When he'd won the Senior Science Award that everyone thought was hers for the taking, she'd been devastated. College was a dream that the award scholarship would've placed within her reach. That she'd eventually made it had lessened the humiliation. Sort of.

But that moment had nothing on what she felt now, admitting this to him.

Ben didn't say anything, didn't look at her, just picked up a chocolate and watched it as he tossed it into the air and caught it. Again and again.

She barreled on. "Listen, I know that you're expected in Sea Breeze at the charity ball on

Saturday, so I figured that if we made an appearance there, everyone would be happy and that would be that. You won't even have to entertain me all week."

He snagged the chocolate out of the air and turned those stormy-gray eyes on her. "No, that won't work."

Panic bubbled in her stomach. "What? Why?"

Ben shook his head. "This 'win a date' contest has been months in the planning. The crew is already here. I—my *employers*—have a lot riding on this. I'm not going to let them down."

He popped the chocolate into his mouth. "I'm sorry you don't want to be here, but since you *did* come, you may as well make yourself comfortable. The first event is dinner in four hours. And it's the National Weather Broadcasters Awards dinner. Formal attire."

"You've got to be kidding me." Maria stalked back to the window, looked out.

He coughed. Cleared his throat. Coughed again.

She didn't look at him. Didn't want to see Ben Storm with the upper hand once again.

A crash sounded behind her. She whirled around.

Ben had knocked a chair over. He fell to the

ground, his hands at his throat. His lips were swollen to twice their normal size, his breath rasping in and out in short, frantic attempts for oxygen.

Maria ran to him, dropping to her knees at his side. He was still conscious but barely. "EpiPen. Do you carry one?"

"Backpack." He forced the words out.

Most people with extreme allergies carried a kit, and he'd been carrying a small, black backpack all day. What had he done with it when they came in? There. By the elevator.

She ran for it, her heart nearly beating out of her chest. Grabbing the bag from the floor, she unzipped it as she ran back to him. *Oh, dear God, his lips are blue. Please help him.*

"Ben!" She dug through the pack.

Throwing things onto the floor as she went, she tossed out a pack of gum, a small spiral notebook and a tattered Bible, nearly crying in relief when her hand closed around the EpiPen.

She tore the top off the case, pulled the pen out and jammed it into his thigh. Within seconds he took a breath. And so did she.

As his color returned to a less scary-pale version of his normal healthy tan, she pressed an albuterol inhaler into his hand. She pushed to her feet and walked into the kitchen for a glass of water. In the other room, she collapsed against the wall, pressing her shaking hands against her mouth.

Ben roused slightly as she got back to his side. She slid a sofa pillow under his head. "Okay?"

He nodded, but didn't open his eyes. She pulled out the Benadryl she'd seen in his backpack and punched out two capsules, placing them in his hand. "Take these."

She slid her arm behind his shoulders and helped him sit up enough to swallow the capsules of lifesaving antihistamine. Her heart rate slowly returning to normal, she peeled off her jacket and threw it on the sofa. "You scared the living daylights out of me. You trying to kill yourself?"

He opened his eyes then, taking a deep breath for the first time in a long few minutes. "No. But I'm pretty sure someone's trying to kill me."

TWO

Ben leaned against the couch, fighting the shakes from the medication. He shot a glance at his date for the weekend. She was so quiet—probably wondering how long it would take her to pack up and get out of Dodge.

Finally Maria shook her head. "Why would you eat that, knowing you have allergies?"

"The resort had instructions about my allergies, just like always. I assumed it would be fine." He let his head drop back on the cushion, only to jerk it up again when he heard her pushing buttons on her cell phone. "What are you doing?"

"Calling the cops. Someone just tried to kill you and nearly gave me a heart attack in the process."

He took the phone from her and pressed End.

"Why did you do that?" Her eyes spit fire, but one lone curl escaped from her ponytail and bounced around her face. For some reason, that made him want to smile.

"Someone broke into my home in Atlanta a couple of weeks ago. Before the police ever got to my house, I got a threatening phone call telling me I'd regret bringing the police into this."

"So? I'm not following. You're not in Atlanta and if someone's trying to kill you, you need police protection." She took her phone from his hand.

She was right, but he couldn't shake the fear that calling attention to this would only escalate things with his stalker. He was putting everything on the line this weekend in order to make the changes he needed to make. But none of it would matter if his family wasn't safe.

What could he do? If he called the police, there could be reprisals that no one could predict. If he didn't, he would still be at risk. Then it occurred to him. "You could do it."

Maria blanched. "I'm not that kind of cop, Ben. I'm a CSI. I work with evidence."

"It would work. Everyone saw the morning show—they know you're my date. No one would suspect you're actually a bodyguard."

"Because I'm *not*." She bounced to her feet, a five-foot-two bundle of repressed energy. "I don't think you're quite getting what I'm saying. I work in a lab."

His eyes were getting heavy, the effects of the epinephrine wearing off and the antihistamine kicking in. It was an effort for his eyes to meet hers and hold them. Like it or not, he needed her. "Please?"

The word hung in the air as his eyes drifted shut.

"Oh, no you don't." Maria shook him. "Ben, wake up. At least get on the couch before you sleep it off."

He shoved upward with his arms and managed to land half of his body on the couch. His eyelids at half-mast, his nonetheless very persuasive eyes met hers and locked on. "Please, Maria? There's more at stake than you know."

His voice slurred, his eyes closing again as he spoke. She blew out a breath and scrubbed her fingers over her eyes. Why was this happening?

Oh, yeah. Gabe and Joe had thrown her under this particular bus and they were going to pay. But the question remained, what did she do now?

She grabbed a faux-fur throw from the back of the couch and tossed it over Ben, pausing for only another second to make sure his breathing was okay before she walked to the table. She wasn't allergic to nuts, so there was no danger for her from the chocolates. She picked one up, broke it in half and sniffed.

Really, unless every single chocolate in this elaborate arrangement had been replaced with one with nuts, how could a killer have known that Ben would pick up one of the chocolates that had peanuts in it?

There was a slight residue on the outside of the chocolates, almost as if they'd been brushed or sprayed with something. She needed to know what. A plastic bag in the kitchen would work as an evidence bag. With Ben's reluctance to get the police involved, she wouldn't call the locals, but she could still have her lab take a look at them.

Maria looked at her watch. The formal event started in three and a half hours. She walked into the rooms he'd called a lockout suite. The decor matched the larger penthouse, but on a slightly smaller scale. Soft instrumental Christmas music played from surround sound speakers she couldn't even see.

Her small overnight bag looked very lonely on the enormous king-size bed. She unzipped it, almost afraid to see what the guys had packed for her. Jeans, a couple of tank tops and her favorite old cashmere sweater were at the top of the pile, which was nice.

Not formal.

She wasn't formal. She was jeans and boots. Dressing up meant lip gloss. Maria dragged a finger across her bare lips. It would take a miracle of epic proportions to pull this off.

A date. And not just any date. What were the guys thinking? She shook her head, frizzy curls flying in all different directions. Oh, she knew what they thought about her—she could handle the truth about herself. She was an independent, occasionally bossy, sometimes cranky, almost always in-charge kind of woman.

The guys had teased her about never having dates. She couldn't fault them on their skills of observation. They were good cops, after all. What they didn't know was that she'd had chances. She'd even taken a few, but when the time came to really make a decision to go for it, she couldn't pull the trigger.

She'd had such a disorganized childhood. Her dad had split when she was pretty young. Not a big deal. It happened to kids all the time—but being bounced from place to place the way she was, her childhood had been chaotic. And yeah, there was still something in her that was afraid of getting left behind by the people who meant the most.

When it really counted, people were unreliable. Chaotic. Science wasn't. It was predictable and safe. Definitive.

The way she saw it, science was God's gift to a messy, messy world. And she used that gift to help other people make sense from their chaos, as science had done for her.

Maria needed science.

But she also knew when science wasn't enough. Right now, she needed help. It was time to call in reinforcements. She paced the room, stopping to finger a branch on a softly glowing Christmas tree. She couldn't make a firm decision until she had all the information.

"Chloe Rollins."

Maria let out the breath she didn't know she'd been holding. "Chloe, I need help. There are all these events and I don't have clothes."

She could hear the smile in Chloe's voice, but of all the cops Maria knew, Chloe was the only one with any fashion sense. "What kind of event is first?"

"A formal." She looked down at her work boots. This was her kind of footwear, not tiny spiked heels with glittery things on them. Blood spatter she could handle. Makeup? Not so much. "Never mind, I don't think I can do this."

"If you *don't* do this, you will never hear the end of it from those guys at the precinct." Chloe was a detective and worked with those same guys, but obviously she was siding with her gender in this fight. "Here's what I want you to do. As soon as you get off the phone with me, call the spa. Have them do…everything. It will be expensive—also worth it. Promise, Maria."

"I promise. And the clothes?" Maria felt like a preteen girl talking to her much cooler, hipper older sister.

"You let me take care of the clothes. I'll see you in two and a half hours. Don't worry." Chloe clicked off.

Don't worry. Maria looked through the open door at the man sleeping on the couch in the living room. Easier said than done.

How many times had Ben told himself the exact same thing when it came to dealing with a stalker who apparently had been targeting him for some time? He'd come very close to dying today.

She walked a little closer. In sleep, the hard planes of Ben's face relaxed. He looked innocent, young. She turned away. The contents of his back-pack still lay tumbled on the floor from her frantic search for the EpiPen. His well-worn Bible was on top of the pile.

Surely he couldn't be all bad, right? Was this who he was? The guy who read the Bible until the pages were slipping from their binding? Her own Bible wasn't nearly as well-used. Maybe she hadn't been reading it as often as she should've.

She smothered a snort. Maybe if she'd been reading hers more often she wouldn't want to smack him with his.

He was right about one thing. He needed help. She still wasn't positive she was the person who needed to give it, but like it or not, she was the person who could.

She slid the key card off the granite countertop and tucked it into her pocket, walked to the elevator and punched the button.

Just what exactly did they do at a spa?

Ben swam through a long, dark tunnel toward a ringing phone. Consciousness came slowly. He punched the button. "Yeah."

"Ben? What is going on? Where are you?" His agent's voice was getting shrill and making Ben's head hurt.

"I'm at the resort, Charlotte. Right where I'm supposed to be." Ben sat up on the couch. His eyes felt like someone had shoved a couple of grapes in with his eyeballs. Maybe in a few minutes he could face opening his eyes, but not yet.

"I saw the broadcast this morning. I can't believe they picked that woman. People have to be interested enough to follow this, Ben. If the ratings don't pick up enough to give them the boost they need—"

"Stop." Maria might not be a supermodel, but she'd saved his life. "Maybe more people will watch because she looks like a normal person, Charlotte. Did you think of that?"

Besides, there was something about her he couldn't quite put his finger on. Those amazing eyes and that spark of intelligence, sure, but there was more. Maybe when his head wasn't so fuzzy he could figure it out.

His agent didn't speak for a moment, a feat in itself. Then she asked, "Are you okay, Ben?"

Ben sighed. "I'm not sure. The stalker got close to me today."

"How close?" His agent's tone warned him that explosion was imminent, but what else could he say?

"Close enough to try to kill me." He held the phone out from his ear. As the shrieks dulled to a lower roar, Ben said, "Can we talk about this?"

"We need to pull the plug on this now." His agent still had a tinge of panic in her voice.

"If I walk away from this event, I walk away from my future." Ben blew out a breath and opened his eyes. The penthouse apartment was almost dark, except for the glowing lights of the Christmas tree. Where was Maria?

"At least let me send someone to look out for you. Someone large, with muscles. And a gun, preferably a very big gun."

Ben chuckled and stood. He swayed on his feet a second, the after-effects of the medication, then walked toward the huge expanse of windows. The sun had dropped into the Gulf of Mexico, but a faint pink glow remained in the western sky.

He turned and faced the room—the fancy-pants suite with its marble floor and enormous Italian chandelier. With just a little bit of luck, he'd be trading it all in on Monday for scarred-up wood floors and a swing set in the backyard. He just needed to keep his priorities straight.

"I've got it covered, Charlotte. I've already engaged a bodyguard." With a few more well-placed reassurances, he managed to hang up with his agent. He switched on a couple of lamps and punched a button that sent the curtains sliding across a hidden track to close out the darkness outside. The door to Maria's suite was closed and behind it he could hear talking as, he hoped, she was getting ready for the evening.

The tux that hung on the back of his bedroom door was one that he'd worn a dozen times or more, but he thought of it now with distaste. He'd much rather be in jeans and a T-shirt, watching a movie and eating microwave popcorn, something some of his coworkers couldn't understand. He knew there were at least a few who would do almost anything to get what he had right now.

Ben had a couple of ideas about who might want to do him harm, but unfortunately he had no proof. What he did have was a feisty CSI on his side, which somehow made him feel less alone.

He picked up his backpack from the floor and began stuffing all the assorted junk back into it, stopping as he got to the Bible. He held it in his hands, reassured by the familiar weight of it. He carried it with him, not as a talisman, but as a reminder and a challenge. A reminder that God was with him even in the tough times, a challenge to be the person God wanted him to be, even in his crazy life. Sometimes it even worked.

Hopefully a steamy shower would wash away the residual sluggishness from his allergy attack. He had a feeling that he would be needing every bit of awareness he could scrounge. He'd very nearly died today in a moment of inattention. He couldn't let that happen again. There were too many people counting on him for Ben to give up that easily.

One weekend. Everything on the line.

THREE

At seven twenty-five, there was a knock on the door. Maria looked in the mirror one more time. She almost didn't recognize the person she saw. She still wasn't quite sure what the stylist had done to her curls to make them so—curly. She'd left the salon with a sackful of hair products.

If she could afford it, she would hire the woman to live with her.

The clothes Chloe brought were fabulous—the fashion-savvy cop had made a whirlwind trip through the BCBG outlet. The shoes were Chloe's own and, while Maria was absolutely sure she would trip every second, she had to admit, if only to herself, that there were some good things about being a girl.

Then there was the makeup artist. He'd brushed on some smoky something around Maria's eyes. That appointment had necessitated another bag of goodies. As Chloe said, the afternoon had definitely not been cheap. But…

Maria looked like a girl. Maybe she'd always known there was a feminine side down inside her somewhere, but it had been well hidden beneath a lab coat and goggles.

She brushed aside her red dress to make sure her small handgun was still tucked into her holster and grinned. Well, maybe not quite so girly.

The knock came again. Maria drew a deep breath, smoothed down her dress and opened the door.

Ben stood in the hall. He smiled when he saw her. "Wow. You look incredible."

She shrugged one shoulder and reached behind her for the wrap that Chloe had insisted she would need. "Thanks, so do you."

He'd been one of *People* magazine's most beautiful people the year before. It was crazy surreal to be here, dressed like this, going to a party with him—a man she would've sworn she didn't like. What she had to figure out was who he really was. Was he Ben Storm the kid she'd known in high school, or was he Ben Storm the television persona? Was that person even real?

What was very real was the fact that someone had tried to kill him. That she was prepared to stand between Ben and that someone if they tried again.

She stepped out the door and saw the television crew behind him. The cameraman winked and waved her forward with one hand as her feet tried to stall out.

Ben took her hand and tucked it into his arm. He leaned in and whispered, "This isn't awkward much, is it?"

She laughed. "A little bit, yeah."

The cameraman jumped on the elevator ahead of them, starting to speak as the red light on the camera went off. "I'll take the elevator down and then send it back for you two. I want to be at the bottom when you get down there. And Ms. Fuentes, you look—amazing."

Amazing wasn't even the word for how she looked. She was absolutely stunning. In fact, if Ben was smart, he would check to make sure he'd picked up his jaw from the floor, where he was pretty sure he'd dropped it when she'd opened the door.

Her red satin dress definitely had wow factor, but it was the transformation in Maria that Ben couldn't get over. She'd done something with her hair and instead of the bouncy tangle she'd had earlier, she wore a long waterfall of loose curls down her back.

The golden eyes that she'd hidden behind chunky sunglasses now looked enormous. Gone was the geeky crime scene investigator. In her place was this gorgeous woman. As the elevator doors closed, she leaned toward him and spoke in his ear, her voice a husky whisper. "You'll need to stay on my left, so I can reach my gun with my right hand."

Ben swallowed hard, her words the dose of cold water he'd needed. She wasn't here to be his arm candy, though she'd certainly qualify. She'd agreed to be his bodyguard. Someone had tried to kill him. He didn't know why it was so hard for him to make that fact sink in. Maybe because it seemed so unbelievable. So extreme.

"I'll try to remember, but if I don't, just give me a pinch and I'll move."

She turned him toward her and reached up to straighten his tie. "You'll be fine, but if you're worried, I could call in some friends—"

"No." He put a hand on her arm, stopping her words. "I'll be fine. Now that we know that someone is gunning for me, we'll be hyperaware. We won't let anyone get close."

As the elevator doors opened, Ben and Maria were spit out into a sea of humanity. Fortunately, because cameras and lights were following them, there was a slight space around them, but he could feel Maria tense beside him and see her eyes as they darted around the room, looking for anything that might be out of the ordinary.

"Get to our table as fast as possible." Maria gazed up at him and said it with a smile, putting herself between him and a guy who was getting a little too close on his right side.

"We're supposed to mingle." But was mingling even possible? He had no real idea who could be out to get him. In a venue like this, with such a crush of people, it would be so easy for someone to attack him.

Someone bumped Maria from behind and she landed hard against his chest. Out of reflex, he wrapped his arms around her, focusing on her eyes.

He took a deep breath as the activity in the room seemed to spin away. "Okay?"

Her smile faded and she blinked. Nodded yes. "There are too many people in here."

When she looked up at him from under her eyelashes, even he believed that she meant she wanted time with him. Then he remembered the cameras.

"Through the double doors to the left. It should

be more quiet in there." He was stopped a couple of times heading to their table, but they finally made it into the banquet hall. As he closed the doors behind him, he waved goodbye to the television audience.

He hadn't expected the stress. He was used to the cameras, but there were so many chances for disaster here.

Maria was finding it hard to concentrate on the conversation at dinner. Her preferred seating position in the room would be in the corner, against the wall. Instead, she and Ben were nowhere near an exit and were surrounded by people. She was beginning to realize that one person couldn't possibly protect another in a situation like this. Waiters rushed in and out. Even the conference attendees didn't seem to be sitting still for very long.

Beside her, one of Ben's coworkers at Weather 24—a guy named Rich according to his name tag—was leaning around her to talk to Ben. "We were back in the Dominican in August. The nuns at the orphanage were so excited about the beds you donated. My wife and I took about two dozen bedsheets. There have been no beds collapsing in the middle of the night in months. And I don't think that any children are sharing beds anymore."

Ben stabbed a piece of broccoli on his plate. "It

helped that you and your wife adopted two of the children."

Rich dug in his pocket. He passed a picture to Maria and pointed. "Ana and Elsa. Aren't they the cutest things you've ever seen?"

They were—bright eyes and pigtails, dressed in matching pink sundresses. "They're precious. How old are they now?"

"Four and seven. We found them when Ben was raising money to send to this orphanage in the Dominican Republic that got damaged in a hurricane two years ago. He got my wife and I involved." He stopped to take a swig of his iced tea. "My wife, Terri, has the biggest heart. Once she saw these little sisters, she knew they were our daughters."

Maria looked at Ben, whose eyes were firmly on his plate of food. Raising money for an orphanage? What else did she not know about Ben Storm? She passed the picture to him.

Ben smiled at the picture of the little girls, then looked up at Rich. "It was a great day for the orphanage when you and Terri got involved."

Across the table, a meteorologist named Mitzi spoke up. "That group in Indonesia you set me up with was incredible, too. I still keep in touch with some of the families we worked with after the tsunami."

Maria caught Ben's eye and raised her eyebrow. He shrugged and rolled his eyes as if he had no idea what Mitzi was talking about.

"I'm still working with the aid group setting up wells in the Sudan after the drought you covered there in 2008," another weather forecaster put in.

Ben scratched his head, his cheeks turning a ruddy color. "You guys—"

"So what's the craziest weather you've ever experienced?" Maria interjected her question as Ben floundered for words. Conversation erupted around the table as each weather geek tried to outdo the other with an over-the-top story.

Ben's eyes met hers across the table. He mouthed thanks, then dove into the table talk with, "There was this one time when I was on assignment in the North Atlantic…"

She hid her smile behind her napkin. He was turning out to be so different than she'd imagined he would be. She'd thought she might be stuck with some kind of prima donna who liked to look at himself in the mirror.

Instead, she got a guy who wore out the pages of his Bible and didn't just report the damage that weather events did to remote places, he actually tried to make a difference for the people affected. She could be attracted to a man like that.

The rubber chicken on the banquet dinner plate suddenly looked even less appealing. Because that idea about Ben was a dangerous, dangerous line of thought. This wasn't real. It was a setup that her stupid coworkers had gotten her into.

There were no feelings involved here, on her part or Ben's. She needed to remember that—think it through. She'd gone beyond classifying Ben as a guy she used to know, or the weatherman she saw on TV sometimes. So what was he, exactly?

The waiter brought a new glass of water and switched it out with Ben's. Laughing at some story that Mitzi was telling about a live report in a hailstorm, Ben reached for it.

"Stop. Don't drink that." The conversation at the table ceased, an awkward, stunned silence falling. All eyes went to her.

But no other glasses at the table tonight had been switched out when empty. They'd been refilled from a central pitcher. She smiled at the waiter. "Could you take that glass away, please?"

The people sitting at the table with them were looking at her like she'd grown a second head. She stage-whispered, "I saw the waiter's finger in the glass."

There were still a few skeptical looks, but Ben handed the glass back to the waiter with a smile. "I'll just keep the one I have, thanks."

Maria made a face and faked a laugh. "Germ phobic—you can't be too careful."

Everyone stared at her for another moment of uncomfortable silence until Rich said, "Yeah, or you'll end up like Ben did that time in Mexico with Montezuma's revenge."

Ben held his stomach and laughed. "Thanks for bringing back that memory."

"What are friends for?" Rich saluted Ben with his iced tea glass.

Maria took a deep breath, the first since she'd seen the waiter try to pass the water to Ben. Watching his back—that's what she was here for. And that's what she needed to remember.

Maybe Ben Storm had turned out to be different than she'd expected, but it didn't matter—couldn't matter. She nudged him into place in her mind in the "protective custody" slot.

Anything else was just her imagination.

Maria shot upright as a scream pierced the air. It wasn't a dream that woke her from the few hours of sleep she'd managed. She picked up her handgun from the bedside table.

She didn't allow a moment's hesitation, just unlocked the door between her suite and the penthouse. Drawing one deep breath and releasing it, she opened the door and stepped through.

Ben was on the floor with a little boy. The two were surrounded by toy cars. Every time Ben would put one in a line, the pajama-clad boy would scream.

Maria had four sisters, each with a brood of their own, so she'd spent a bunch of time around kids. She pegged this one to be around four. And since Ben obviously wasn't in trouble, she turned to go back to her suite, wondering where in the world Ben had picked up a preschooler since she'd said good-night to him, six hours earlier.

"I hope we didn't wake you." Ben's velvety smooth news voice stopped her as she reached for the doorknob.

She turned back, took a deep breath and tucked her hair behind her ears. "I'm used to getting up early."

"You're welcome to join us, although if you want quiet, you'd be better off barricading yourself in your suite. My son is ready for breakfast and waiting is not exactly his strong point."

"I'm hungry, Dad." The boy poked Ben with a car.

Ben looked at Maria, amusement in the wry curve of his lips.

She swallowed hard and turned away, but she didn't run back to her suite, instead placing her weapon in a high cabinet where the little one wouldn't be able to reach it. With a smile, she crossed the room and folded her legs underneath her to sit on the floor. "Hi, bud, I'm Maria."

Blondy-brown hair fell over the little kid's eyes as he dropped his head, burying it in Ben's armpit.

"Hey, Capo, we've talked about this. What can you say to Maria?"

A very muffled greeting came from Ben's shoulder area.

Maria grinned. "Capo?"

"His name is Caden, but his mother played the guitar and she used to say that he was her perfect pitch." Ben's eyes had a sheen to them and Maria looked at the cars on the floor.

"Is there a secret to how you're lining them up?"

"Yeah, I line them up and he screams when I put them in the wrong place," Ben said with a laugh, the affection in his eyes sweet as he looked at the little boy. And if she'd built an ice wall around the section of her heart named Ben Storm, as she watched him with Caden, another layer melted.

Caden walked to the window and placed his palms flat against the glass, looking out at the ocean.

"Caden's on the autistic spectrum. He's made a ton of progress in therapy—" Ben shrugged. "He doesn't adjust to change well. The nanny called last night and said that he was freaked that I wasn't home, so we thought it might be best to bring him over. I know it's not ideal, given the situation."

"No." Maria watched Caden reach out to touch an ornament on the tree and check himself, looking at his dad. "But if he stays in the suite and his nanny is aware of what's going on, we should be able to minimize the risk."

Ben's gray eyes were soft with worry as he said, "He's been through so much change lately. It's been rough on him. He'll settle down by this afternoon, I hope. His nanny is in the other adjoining suite, putting his comforter on the bed and setting up some of his things."

"You have custody?" She wrapped her arms around her legs, pulling her knees in.

"His mom died in a car accident two years ago. It's been tough. And it's the reason I'm leaving Weather 24 after this weekend."

She nodded, watching Caden trail his fingers down the long glass expanse, then she snapped her gaze back to Ben's as his words sank in. "You're what?"

"Caden needs a full-time dad. My job with Weather 24 has me on the road constantly. You heard stories last night—I follow weather events all over the world." He shrugged, his face carved into a mask of resolve. "I can do the weather at six and ten on the local news channel and be home in between to tuck my son into bed."

Maria nudged one of the cars into line. A small voice piped up beside her. "It doesn't go there."

She looked into his very serious big blue eyes. "Okay, Mr. Mechanic, where does it go?"

He giggled and plopped on his dad's lap. "Did you hear that, Dad? She called me Mr. Mechanic. Mechanics work on cars."

Caden chortled some more as he moved the red car she'd put in the line and put a black one in its place. He picked up an orange car and looked at Maria, his little mouth pursed. "You can put this one by the black one."

Ben's wide eyes told her that she'd passed some kind of major test. She held her hand out for the orange car and very, very carefully placed it next to the black one, making sure the wheels were lined up just right.

When Caden nodded his approval, she breathed a silent sigh of relief. He was adorable. "You know, Caden, I work in a lab doing experiments. I get really annoyed when people touch my stuff, too."

His dark eyelashes flipped up and he gave her a suspicious look. "You do science?"

"Yep."

He picked up the red car and handed it to her. "Are you smart?"

"Yes." She placed the red car in the line, again being very careful to get it spaced just right. "So are you."

"Yep." As he placed the next car in the line, a young woman came out of a door to the right of the living area. Maria hadn't noticed it before, but it was another lockout suite. Apparently, one could rent the penthouse unit they were in now, or the entire floor, if they were all put together.

"Hey, Caden, I got our rooms all set up. Are you ready for some oatmeal?"

"I want pancakes." His blue eyes went from one care provider to another, testing the water.

Ben ignored Caden's words, instead turning to Maria. "Maria, I'd like for you to meet our most amazing nanny and therapist, Julia. Julia, this is my friend, Maria.

"Pancakes!" Caden's voice was a little louder, a little more frustrated.

Ben lifted his son into his arms as he stood. "Julia fixed oatmeal for breakfast. You can have pancakes when we get home."

"Want pancakes." Caden's bottom lip poked out and might even have quivered a little bit. "With blueberries."

"I know, bud. Let's go have some yummy oatmeal. We'll put some brown sugar in it." Ben looked at the nanny, who nodded. "Maria?"

"Thanks, but no. I just need coffee." She was already backing away. Cowardly of her, yes, but watching Ben Storm with his little boy made him all the more human to her.

As Maria poured her cup of coffee, her cell phone rang. She walked back to her suite of rooms, finding the phone beside her bed.

Chloe Rollins didn't waste any words when Maria answered. "I got the lab report this morning on those candies you gave me last night. Someone definitely tried to kill your weatherman. There was a very fine coating of peanut dust on the candies."

The warmth of the cup did nothing to warm

Maria's suddenly chilled fingers. "Thanks, Chloe. I guess that means it's time for me to get some answers."

Another trip across the large penthouse to the other lockout suite and she was right where she didn't want to be, watching Ben be a daddy to his son.

Maria was out of her element. Kids, great— she had a dozen nieces and nephews she adored. Adults, great. People in danger, she could deal. Put all three together in this appealing package and she was struggling to remember that this—her being a part of this, anyway—wasn't real. She was just one very small, relatively insignificant piece of Ben's plan.

Chaos. She needed science.

"You changed your mind about organic steel-cut oats?"

Ben's smile faded as he took in her expression. "What's up?"

"We need to talk."

Ben stood and grabbed a jacket off the counter with a pointed look at Caden. "Let's take a walk."

Maria hesitated. Ideally, she would want a whole team of trained protection personnel for an outside detail. But as cold as it was, there would be few beachcombers this early, making it easier for her to identify a threat.

Now that she knew the candies had been deliberately tampered with, it was even more vital that she stay alert. Ben's life depended on it.

FOUR

The surf tossed and rolled, the breeze chilly. Ben pulled his windbreaker up around his neck and turned to Maria, who was scanning the resort behind them. "You were really great with Capo this morning. Thanks."

"I like kids. They mean what they say." She smiled, but it didn't reach her eyes.

"He's come a long way. Right after his mother died, I started realizing there was a problem. With autism, early intervention is essential. He does hours of therapy every day, which he mostly thinks is play, thanks to Julia." He reached for Maria's arm and turned her to face him. "What's going on?"

The wind tossed her hair and she pushed it back with an impatient hand. "We found peanut dust on the candies. It's no longer a possibility that you ate something by accident. Someone tried to kill you. I need you to tell me everything."

The sudden constriction in his chest had nothing to do with peanut dust and everything to do with the knowledge that someone really was out to get him.

He shook his head and walked away. It wasn't that he wouldn't talk about it. He just didn't know where to start.

Maria stepped into place beside him, stuffing her hands into the pockets of her jeans. "Why don't you tell me about the first contact?"

"The first was a note about two years ago, shortly before my wife's car accident. It was on the back of a black-and-white photo of Lindsay and Caden at the park. All it said was, 'Are they safe?'"

Her eyebrows drew together, golden-sparked eyes serious. "What did you do?"

"Warned Lindsay, got a monitored alarm system, told security at the network. But her accident wasn't very long after that first contact and, after that, I didn't think about anything but surviving one day at a time with Capo for a long, long time." He stopped, kicked at the sand.

He could see Maria's wheels turning as she rubbed her hands together. "Did you tell the police who investigated your wife's accident about the note?"

"Yes, her death—" there was still the barest

hesitation as he said it "—was ruled accidental. She ran into a tree."

A small frown appeared at the corner of Maria's mouth. "What next?"

"I was fighting for custody of Capo, trying to keep my job from the vultures who would try to take it every time I had to take a day off or turn down a trip. You can't imagine." Even now, the memories of that time ran together in a blur.

"Was it your in-laws that wanted Caden?"

"In a sense. He'd just been diagnosed with autism. My brother-in-law and his wife petitioned the court, arguing that an intact and stable family would be better for Caden than living with a grief-stricken father who traveled most of the time for his job." Ben scrubbed a hand over his eyes, rubbing the memory away. If only it were really that easy.

"Is that when you hired Julia?"

He nodded. "I needed someone who could help with his therapeutic needs but also give him continuity of care when I travel. It's been so worth it."

The temperature was dropping quickly, the way it sometimes did this time of year. Maria blew into her hands, a futile attempt at warming them. His gear was made for all weather—he wrapped his warm hands around her cold ones and pulled her in, sheltering her from the wind.

He smiled down into Maria's wide eyes. "I've been dreading this weekend ever since the powers-that-be came up with the idea. But you've made it really easy, despite all the drama. Thanks."

Her teeth bit into her full lower lip, but she shook her head. "Not a problem."

She stepped away from him, but he kept one hand as they turned to walk back toward the resort. Small and feminine, her hand completely disappeared into his until she pulled it out to swap sides with him.

"My job is pretty high profile. It's silly, really. I'm a meteorologist, just like a lot of other people who predict the weather on television. But there are those couple of guys who hate my guts and would love to take the job away from me. Do I think one of them would resort to murder? No, but what do I know?" He blew out a frustrated breath.

"Do they know that you're leaving?"

He shook his head. "I can't tell anyone until the official announcement. I signed a contract that effectively binds my hands. I'll announce it tomorrow night, and then do my last weather report Saturday night after the Christmas ball."

Maria was quiet for two or three swishes of the

waves. "Once you make the announcement, if it's a coworker wanting your job, this should stop. If it's a coworker that has developed an unhealthy obsession, it might not. I'll need their names."

She seemed so much bigger than her five-foot-two frame, a look of intense concentration on her face as she watched the people on the beach. One loopy curl bounced over her shoulder in the breeze.

As he nodded, he realized she hadn't swapped sides with him because she wanted to be farther from the water, or even because she wanted an excuse to stop holding hands with him. She'd taken the high side because she was putting her body between him and danger.

The beach no longer seemed like a neutral place to have a serious talk. It seemed like a place where danger was all too easy to overlook. And from the way she'd positioned herself, danger would have to go through her to get to him. He couldn't let that happen. "Let's get inside, out of the wind."

He hadn't missed the gun in her hand when she'd come out of her suite this morning in her sweatpants, her hair flying. She'd been thinking of his safety—and then, putting the gun in the high cabinet, she'd been thinking of his son's.

When he'd asked her to stay, he'd only been

concerned about what it would mean for him if the date weekend fell through. He'd been so focused on getting through the weekend that he hadn't even thought about her—her safety. He may not think like a cop, but he did think like a man, and right now there was no way he was letting her take a hit for him.

As they climbed the wooden steps of the board-walk leading to the resort, Ben reached for Maria's hand again. "I don't think we should go through with this."

Maria stopped, the question on her face—why the abrupt turnaround?

Before he could reply, lights flashed on. "Looks like our lucky twosome have been for a walk on the beach this morning. How was it?"

The cameraman held the microphone to Maria. She stared at it for a second and, just as Ben started to reach for it, she took it and smiled. "I'm sure you can probably tell from my red nose that the beach is cold. The wind is from the north at around fifteen to twenty miles per hour and the temperature is dropping. Probably forties right now, would you say, Ben?"

The cameraman chuckled as he took the mike back. "I think you should be worried about your job, Ben. She's a natural. Want to fill us in on the rest of the country?"

Studying the daily forecast was part of his routine, even when he was away from the office. Despite everything else going on, he could always report the weather. "Maria's right, here in Northwest Florida temperatures are chilly, mid to low forties, dropping into the upper thirties by this afternoon. Around the country, an early snow is the big weather event. School kids from Colorado all the way to Tennessee are celebrating with a snow day. These storms will be moving toward the eastern seaboard tomorrow."

Ben's easy on-camera smile belied the turmoil he felt inside—the pain of dredging up memories mixed with a growing admiration for Maria. But he'd learned a long time ago that feelings had no place on the air. "And that's your quick and dirty weather report. I'm Ben Storm in Destin, Florida."

The producers would take that short sound bite and put copy around it. The anchors would put it in context, giving the viewing audience a reminder of what Ben and Maria were doing in Desin and a teaser for when they would see them next.

"We're clear." The cameraman high-fived Ben. "See you a little later tonight?"

"Yep. We're on the schedule for a pre-event private dinner, I think." Out of the corner of his eye, Ben saw Maria shiver and he put his arm around her.

"You did great on camera. Not everyone can be natural like that." Ben turned toward the resort as the camera guys moved on to get some stock footage of the beach.

He was a natural on camera, but he'd never expected to be anything but an on-air meteorologist, forecasting the weather just like any other one. It had been a shock to start getting attention for his looks. When that magazine had called attention to him, a whole new kind of insanity had begun, with paparazzi following him.

Maria was quiet as they rode the elevator up to the penthouse. He didn't blame her. His life was a mess and she'd landed squarely in the middle of it.

Finally she stopped in front of him and held on to the lapels of his coat. "You didn't get me into this, my coworkers did," she said. "And now that I'm here, there's no way I'm letting Caden grow up without a dad if I can help it. Got it?"

He nodded, a grin crinkling the corners of his eyes. "Yes, ma'am."

"Good."

Ben called after her. "See you at five for an early dinner?"

"Write down the names." Her eyes were warm and her smile generous, especially when he still knew he didn't deserve it.

Maria was dialing her cell phone before she had even opened the door to her suite. When Chloe answered, she filled her in on the two coworkers. "We'll need to check them out, find out where they were the last couple of days. If either of them is at this conference, we'll have to get the police to take them in for questioning."

"I'll get on it as soon as you text me the names.."

"There's one more thing, Chloe. Ben said the threats started before his wife was killed in a wreck. It was ruled accidental, but…"

"You want to see the report. Okay, I'll hunt it down and text you when the fax is headed your way. Is that it?"

"Yes—no. There's this dinner thing."

Laughter pealed through the cell phone. "Wear the black velvet and the heels with the rhinestone clasp."

Maria used the bag of tricks that the ladies in the salon had showed her and ended up with a loose pile of ringlets on her head. The black-velvet sheath dress was devastatingly simple, with a scoop neck and long, narrow sleeves.

Chloe was a genius.

Her phone buzzed on the nightstand—the text message she'd been waiting for. Pages began to spew out of the fax machine on the desk in the sitting area.

Her crime scene investigator brain itched to get into that file, but she had other commitments now.

She opened the door to the penthouse, clutching a black satin evening bag with her weapon tucked inside. Ben met her in the living room, beside the Christmas tree. She smiled as she saw the line of toy cars still in the exact order where Caden had left them earlier.

Dressed in khaki pants and a blue blazer, Ben was tieless in his crisp white shirt. "I hope you don't mind. I decided dinner on the balcony might be nicer than a restaurant with the cameras around. They'll still be in and out to film us, but for the most part we'll have our privacy."

In that short couple of hours, he'd transformed the balcony. Small trees of differing heights twinkled. An exquisite table was set and soft strings played Christmas music in the background.

"It's beautiful. But, uh, Ben, shouldn't a meteorologist be aware that it's beastly cold outside?"

"Give it a try."

She stepped out the open door into warm air, even warmer than inside the room. Gas patio heaters lined the edge of the balcony. She looked back at Ben. "You score ten for use of heaters."

"Thanks. The guys will be here in a minute, but I wanted you to see it first. They'll get your reaction—again—and tape us being seated and a little cheesy conversation. Then they'll duck out and we'll be able to eat dinner in peace. We won't see the cameras again until dessert. Okay with you?"

"Sure. This experience hasn't been nearly as horrifying as I thought it would be."

Ben smothered a laugh as he waved in the camera crew.

After a quick sound bite for the cameras, she and Ben were seated on the balcony. Even sixteen floors up, the soft sounds of the ocean were a soothing and perfect backdrop.

With the appetizer, Ben asked, "So how does one become a crime scene investigator?"

The question brought images like a hundred fast-play slides through her mind. She closed her eyes and prayed for God's peace—that she could use the skills He'd given her to catch the men and women who did these crimes and put them away, and that she could live with herself when she was done.

Then the image of Ben's tattered Bible came to her mind. Maybe he'd been searching for peace, too. She looked into Ben's eyes and knew that it was time to tell him the truth. Somehow she thought he'd understand.

"It was part accident, part design, I think. I didn't have the money to go to college full time, so I worked at the sheriff's office during the day and went to classes at night. The more I worked with the sheriff's department, the more I realized there was a real place for science and technology in gathering evidence. So, I decided to major in chemistry and physics. Later I got another degree in criminology."

"All on your own? That's incredible."

"My mom died when I was in junior high school. I lived with my aunt, who was great, but she didn't have any money. I did get some scholarships, but the big one that would've sent me to college was won by someone else."

He lifted his gaze from his salad to stare at her, his eyes narrowed.

She took a sip from a water goblet on the fancy

table. "I realized recently that it was my own fault. I let my grades slip when things were going on with my family. If I hadn't, I probably would've gotten the scholarship. But you wouldn't be sitting here."

"You—you're Maria Fuentes. High school Maria Fuentes." His voice held just a hint of accusation.

"Yes." Maria poked lettuce with her fork, calmly took a bite.

When he continued to stare at her, she motioned to his plate. "You can eat now."

Ben still didn't move. "I don't know what to say."

"My aunt had this cross-stitch on her wall. I always thought it was really cheesy, but now—I think it's true. It said, 'Wherever God closes a door, he opens a window.'"

"Your window was crime scene investigation?"

She smiled. "I don't know if you've noticed this because I've been on my best behavior, but I'm very tenacious. That quality makes me a good fit for CSI. I like my life."

"Why didn't you tell me?" He still hadn't taken another bite of his salad.

That was a good question. Why hadn't she told him? "I remembered losing that scholarship as being so humiliating. I guess it was, to a seventeen-year-old."

"And look at you now."

She laughed. "Yes, because I always wear velvet and diamonds."

Their private dinner passed with quiet conversation, laughter and animated talk of new technologies. For each of them as teenagers, science had been an escape. Now it was common ground.

As the coffee was served, Ben stood. "I need to go tuck Caden into bed. You can come, if you like."

Cops weren't scared of cute little boys—or their handsome dads.

Maria followed Ben to Caden's suite. Like hers, it had a small kitchen and a private sitting room. Unlike hers, there were baskets of toys and little trucks. On the bed was a spread covered with colorful freight trains.

"Story time, Daddy!" Caden bounced on the bed, his fresh-from-the-bath hair sticking out from his head.

"One story, Capo, because it's time for you to go to sleep." Ben held out his hand. Caden handed him his favorite book.

As Ben read, using silly voices and making bug-eyed faces, Caden giggled. Then slowly, his eyes got heavy as he played with the floppy ears of his stuffed bunny. He was so adorable, obviously bright. She couldn't imagine what it must've been like for Ben to see that bright light trapped inside Caden's little body and be afraid he would never be able to communicate.

They were so blessed.

As Ben finished the book, Caden held up his arms for a hug. Ben hugged.

The nanny, Julia, hugged.

"Her, too." Caden's voice, so sleepy seconds ago, piped up from the bed.

Ben's gray eyes were apologetic, asking for her understanding. "You don't have to—but it's sort of a ritual now. Hugs from everyone before bed."

"It's fine, Ben. I've got at least a dozen nieces and nephews—I'm familiar with bedtime rituals." She sat on the edge of the bed. "'Night, Caden. I'll see you in the morning?"

He nodded. "Sing?"

She looked at Ben, who shrugged. So this was a departure from the ritual. "I have a niece about your age who comes to stay with me sometimes. She likes to hear 'Twinkle, Twinkle' before she goes to sleep."

"Sing," Caden commanded.

"All right, Captain Caden. You lay your head on the pillow and I'll sing you a song."

Maria sang the words to the simple nursery rhyme. In a few seconds, she felt a warm hand nestle into hers. She was having a little trouble catching her breath as she squeezed the little hand.

She looked at Ben, whose eyes were wide, and thought, *God, I could really use some air about now. Do You think You could open a window?*

FIVE

Coffee on the terrace with the film crew was less than stellar for Ben. It was a little hard to keep his mind on saying the right thing when his insides were all jumbled up. He kept replaying in his head that single moment when his four-year-old had put his chubby little hand in Maria's.

For a normal kid, maybe that wasn't such a big thing, but for a kid like Caden—it was huge. It hadn't been so long ago when doctors were warning him it might be unrealistic to expect affection from Caden. The reality was that Caden was not only capable of showing affection, he did—often. But usually only with family, which made those moments with Maria all the more remarkable.

As the film crew packed up and left, he joined Maria at the balcony rail. The breeze was stiff, yet she leaned into it, her eyes closed, lashes a lacy semicircle on her cheeks.

She shivered.

Ben pulled off his sport coat and draped it around her shoulders, pulling her close into his side. "You're an incredible woman, Maria Fuentes."

"I bet you say that to all the girls."

"That's just it. There are no other girls." Yeah, he said it out loud and he probably should have been embarrassed, but he wasn't. It was freeing to have her know him—and she did. She knew his past and she most definitely knew his present. He wasn't sure about the future yet, but now that he'd found her he wasn't sure he wanted to let go of her.

She laughed softly. "I bet you say *that* to all the girls, too."

"You know what I find the most incredible? You've seen me at my absolute worst. Literally gasping for air. You've seen what my life is like, how hard we have to work every day just to achieve a little bit of normal. And yet, you didn't run screaming from the building." He tugged her closer to see what she would do. She didn't move away. Maybe she snuggled a little closer.

"And my hair's not on fire and I'm not in need of medication. Contrary to what you might think, Ben, your life is not that weird compared to what I see on a regular basis."

He turned her to face him, searching her

beautiful golden-brown eyes. "Are you still sorry your coworkers sent your name in for this contest?"

Maria made a face, contemplating her answer—and his stomach twisted. "They're still going to pay. But how could I be sorry?"

Sliding his fingers into the hair at the nape of her neck, he cupped her face in his hands. He kept forgetting how small she was, how beautiful. It snuck up on him. He placed his lips at her hairline by the temple and felt her tremble.

He wrapped his arms around her and pulled her close, just holding her.

His phone beeped in his pocket. He sighed. "I have to go."

She stepped out of his arms and slid his coat off her shoulders. "I'll be here when you get back. And Ben, I know I can't go with you to this one, but please—be careful."

With Ben at a meeting, Maria changed into flannel PJs and pulled the file from the fax machine. Evidence was empirical—it made sense, even when people's actions didn't.

She sipped her cup of coffee and tried not to think about how long it would take Ben to get back from his meeting of weather forecasters. He'd decided to go it alone rather than call attention to himself by having her along. She still wasn't sure she agreed that it was the safest action to take.

From her first cursory glance at the reports, Ben's wife's car wreck looked like an accident. She'd been on her way home from an out-of-town meeting. Her power steering had failed as she went too fast around a curve. Unable to keep the car on the road, she hit a tree before she could adequately slow down. The car exploded on impact.

The accident had taken place on a back road in Georgia and was investigated by the local cops, who had documented the scene. Pictures had low resolution over a fax, but as she studied the pages, what happened that night became more and more clear.

The elevator chimed softly. Ben stepped off, his navy sport coat draped over his arm. Even tired and worried, he was so handsome it was ridiculous. When he caught sight of her on the sofa, he smiled.

The slow spread across his face started an equal spread of warmth in her belly. She leaned into the cushions, wrapping her old gray sweater tighter around her. She hadn't often felt in danger—she'd been taught from an early age to defend herself, but how did a girl defend herself from that smile?

"Work?" He dropped onto the couch beside her and gestured at the papers on the coffee table.

She drew in a breath, not sure how to tell him what she suspected. "Not exactly."

"Those are evidence reports, right?" He reached for the papers on the table, then stopped with his hand in mid-air. "May I?"

"It's your wife's accident report."

His hand dropped to his knee. "What?"

She shrugged, the warmth replaced by a queasy insecurity. "After we talked earlier, I wanted to check it out, make sure the investigators didn't miss anything."

He stood, paced to the wide windows, where she could still see the twinkling patio lights from their intimate dinner. "I don't know what made you think you had the right."

His words were toneless, very unlike the Ben she'd come to know. But she'd touched a raw place—and he was protecting himself, and probably Caden, too, in the only way he knew how. She couldn't let it get to her. "It's what I do, Ben."

Even knowing why he reacted that way, it hurt. She retreated to evidence, her comfort zone. "There are some things that you might want to see in this report."

"Maria, I don't know how to make it any more

clear that I don't want to discuss my wife's death. It was a horrible accident." His eyes were full of pain, even after two years, and she didn't blame him. The mother of his child had been killed.

"It wasn't an accident," she blurted. "At least, I don't think it was."

"Are you serious? You haven't physically seen the evidence, and from a report you can put together something that the cops couldn't and didn't?" He shook his head. "No. I don't believe it."

She stood and laid the pages out on the coffee table. "You're a scientist. I know it's hard to be objective here, but follow the evidence with me. Look at the damage report to the car. There's damage on the driver's side of the car that isn't consistent with her running into the tree and the car exploding. It looks more like someone forced her off the road."

Ben whipped his head up to meet her eyes. "Someone did this deliberately?"

"The report says that the seal on her power steering was stripped. I don't think that's a coincidence. If someone forced her off the road, with no power steering she might not have had the skills to avoid a crash."

"She was *murdered?*" He jolted to his feet and

paced away, only to turn back, the awful truth sinking in.

"The police report says that the driver's side damage means she probably bounced off another tree. But if she had, it would've affected the trajectory. And look at the tire tracks in this photograph. Straight tracks down the hill. There's no way she hit another tree."

His hands turned up in a position of surrender. "I don't even know what to say. I never imagined that she might've been—I never imagined it."

Maria stacked the pages and closed the file. "We need another list. One with names of people who might have something against either you or your wife."

His horrified eyes met hers. "I was supposed to be in the car with her that night. She'd been speaking about her charity at a Rotary Club meeting in that little town and I was going to go with her, but Capo was fussing with the sitter. He had a cold and wouldn't settle down. I stayed home."

Her heart went out to him, but she couldn't give him sympathy, couldn't allow him to fall apart. It was too important that they get to the bottom of this. "Whoever it was tried to kill both of you. They didn't know you weren't in the car until it was too late."

"I can't believe this. How could the police miss it?"

"Easy. They believed it was an accident so they looked for confirmation. They saw the unexplained dents and rationalized them away. It happens."

He turned back to her, his skin ashen. "I'm sorry, Maria. I just can't take this in. Do you mind if we talk about it tomorrow?"

"Tomorrow will be fine, Ben. Let it process."

"I'm addressing the conference in the morning at ten."

"You should have a whole team protecting you at an event like this. I could call a few friends—"

"No. It would leak to the media and this can't become about me and a stalker. It has to be about the date, about the network and the future."

She paced the room, too, ending up by the Christmas tree, its peaceful beauty doing nothing to calm savage nerves. "I need to be where I can see the room tomorrow."

"What if I bring you up and introduce you as the woman who survived a date with me? We'll make it funny." Ben walked to the tree and reached for her hand, sliding her fingers through his. "I'm thankful you're here—that you're walking through this craziness with me."

"Yeah, I'm thankful, too." Her dry tone made him chuckle and he put his arms around her.

"I'm serious, Maria. I know this weekend has been anything but fun for you, but in spite of everything, being with you makes it bearable. I said it earlier and I meant it—you're beautiful, inside and out. I never expected that."

Her heart was rattling inside her chest. She laced her fingers tighter into his. "I think you're overwhelmed by all that's happened. Maybe you're more emotional than usual. When you take a step back, you'll realize that you needed a friend, and I was here."

Very gently, he tipped her chin up and brushed his lips across hers. Her breath caught in her chest, unwanted moisture springing to her eyes.

He tilted his head back and looked at her again, his eyes narrowed. "Nope, sorry. That didn't feel like friends to me."

She pulled her hand free. Flattening both hands on his chest, she gave him a gentle push. *"Tú eres un sabihondo.* I'll see you in the morning."

He chuckled as he backed away from her. "You know, I've spent a lot of time in Latin American countries. I know you just called me a know-it-all."

"Yeah, yeah. Get out of here, weather boy."

As he disappeared into his bedroom, with shaking hands she gathered the papers from the accident report and walked back to her suite. It took three tries to get the key card to work but finally it did.

There had been so much change in such a small space of time. Her mind was reeling. *Dear God, what should I do?*

People weren't scientific. How did she deal with this, with these feelings for Ben, which were getting stronger every time she was around him?

It was hard to put a name to them, they were many and varied, but she could identify the most pressing. Fear. She'd watched her friends and siblings fall in love and get married, have children. She'd never dared to even imagine that such life could be for her. Happily-ever-after was a fairy tale that happened to other people.

But Ben made her dream, which seemed to her a surefire recipe for disaster.

Ben had the whole ballroom rocking with laughter. He was pretty sure that it was the story about the bee stinging him on camera that won them over, though the video of the slide into a mud-filled canal during a typhoon in Japan had been epic. He waited for the laughter to die down. "Working for Weather 24 has been an adventure every day. *Weather* is an adventure. I love it.

"I wouldn't do this job if I didn't have a passion for the weather and how it affects our lives—our basic human condition. We report the weather, yes, but we also live it. In doing so, we have the rare opportunity to bring the world closer together. The mother in Little Rock can experience what's going on in Indonesia. The businessman in Prague can understand the tourist industry in Mazatlan and the climate that fuels it."

His heart pounded. He was so close, so incredibly close to finishing this. Ben's gaze connected with Maria's. She was standing to his left at the corner of the stage. Her hair was pulled back into a low, smooth ponytail. In a few, short days, she'd come to mean a lot to him, and six months ago he couldn't have imagined that he would ever have feelings for another woman besides his wife.

Everything changed.

"I've loved every minute of my job with Weather 24, but it's time for me to move on." The audible gasp from the floor amused him. Truthfully, he would've reacted the same way ten years ago when he was first starting out. What kind of idiot would leave a sweet job like his voluntarily?

He looked at his notes and then set them aside,

deciding to talk impromptu to the men and women, many of whom he'd known for years. "My friends, I would say this to you. Be passionate about life, share your love and don't be afraid to reinvent yourself."

Ben picked up his notes and left the podium as the room erupted in applause. Cameras flashed. He reached Maria's side and took her arm.

"Other side." She moved to partially shield him from the crowd. Clearly uneasy, her eyes darted back and forth in the crowded ballroom. "We've got to get out of here."

Something popped and a vase on the stage exploded, sending shards of glass flying, water and flowers spilling onto the stage floor.

Where there had been applause, screams now echoed. People knocked over chairs to get out of the ballroom.

Ben couldn't make sense of the chaos. Maria stopped pretending to walk and gripped his arm, nearly dragging him out double doors into a service hall that ran behind the ballroom.

After they cleared the room, Maria didn't slow down. She hustled him down the hall toward more doors, her gun in her hand.

"What was that?"

"Someone took a shot at you, Ben." She didn't

pause at the doors to the emergency stairs, just whipped through them.

Her words sunk in. "Someone—wait. You said someone shot at me?"

"Yes, Ben. Keep moving. We've got to get to the service elevator, but I want you off this floor first." She ran behind him on the steps, never faltering even in those three-inch heels.

He reached for the door handle to the next floor.

"Stop." Her voice was low and cool—he didn't question her authority. "Me first."

She had a gun—he wasn't going to argue.

"Stay quiet and move fast. We're turning left outside the door. The service elevator is at the end of the hall."

"How do you know?" He would've been completely lost by now.

"Shh." She opened the door and went through first, motioning him to follow. Silently, they made their way down the hall. Almost at the end, they heard excited voices.

"Hurry." Maria's whisper was a hiss near his ear. She pulled open the door to the maintenance area and shoved him through it. He heard her take an audible breath as she pushed the button for the elevator. "Get behind me."

He took a breath to argue.

"Do it." She didn't look back, but held her gun in the classic police stance, aimed at the place the doors would open.

The elevator chimed as it stopped and as the doors cracked open, Ben stopped breathing. Empty. He breathed again. "How did you know where this elevator was?"

"I did some exploring the first day we were here, while you were zonked out from the antihistamines." On the elevator, Maria swiped the card through the slot that would authorize the elevator to take them to the penthouse. "We've got to get you away from this hotel. Too easy for someone to hide here."

"We've got to get Caden out of here." When her eyes widened, he said, "They drove here in my car, but I don't want to take the chance that they could be in danger if they're on their own."

She took a deep breath, readjusting her plans in her mind. "How much do you trust your helicopter pilot?"

He thought back to all the times that the pilot had been in dangerous weather with him and had saved his hide as they'd cut it knife-edge thin to leave safely. "I trust him with my life."

"Call him, but tell him not to tell anyone,

except whoever he has to clear it with legally to fly here."

"Got it." The elevator doors slid open into the maintenance closet on the penthouse floor. Maria exited first, but the thought that something might've happened to his son propelled Ben forward.

He didn't have to worry long. Caden was sitting under the Christmas tree with his cars, making motor sounds as he raced them in a circle around him.

Julia looked up from the sink in the kitchen. "Hi. Hot chocolate, anyone?"

Maria turned and slid her weapon into the holster under her jacket. Her look spoke volumes, but what she said to Ben was, "I'll go finish packing. You need to do the same."

"I know. Let me talk to Julia."

Maria went to her suite and shoved all the beautiful new clothes into a bag. The hair products and makeup went into another, smaller bag. Realistically, she knew that they might have to send for their things. Suitcases were a little bulky for running from bad guys who were shooting at them.

Ben came to the door. "We have a little problem with the helicopter. Caden can't ride in it. He would go ballistic—it's too loud, even with headphones."

"Okay, we'll have to go to plan B. We'll get you to safety." As she saw his face, she went to him at the door. "We'll think of another way, don't worry."

"Cars, Daddy?" A small head peered around Ben's leg.

Ben picked Caden up, holding him close. "Five minutes of cars, and then we have to help Julia pack." His voice drifted back as he carried Caden into the living room of the penthouse suite.

Maria dialed the number of the police lieutenant who had gotten her into this mess. "Gabe, it's Maria. I need your help."

SIX

Two hours later, Maria, Ben, Caden and Julia stepped onto the elevator. If anyone were to get on at a lower floor, on one side of the elevator they would see a family of three dressed for a trip to the indoor pool. On the other side of the cab, Maria would pass as a teenager, texting on her cell phone, hot-pink ball cap pulled low over her eyes and ear buds in her ears.

Over her shoulder, Julia had a beach bag with Caden's cars and a few snacks for the trip. The plan was for Chloe to bring the rest of their things once they were safely on the road.

On the sixth floor, Chloe got on the elevator with them, opposite Maria. Dressed as a uniformed firefighter, she had a clipboard and a walkie-talkie—just doing inspection.

At the third floor, Gabe, dressed in a business suit, got on the elevator. He didn't even glance at the little "family," checking his watch instead.

Maria tucked her cell phone in her back pocket as Chloe and Gabe got off at the lobby. Maria would ride down to the parking garage with Ben, Caden and Julia and put them in a vehicle that was waiting by the elevator doors. Blowing out a breath, she shook her cold fingers and caught Ben looking at her.

She shot him a wink and went back to listening over her earpiece to Gabe talking to Joe Sheehan in the parking garage. If all went according to plan, they should be out of here in two minutes. Gabe would jump in from the stairwell and Joe would follow in a marked cop car.

Those fifteen or twenty seconds that they would be exposed would be the most dangerous of the whole trip. But Joe Sheehan would be on one side of them and she would be on the other side. It would be fine. It had to be fine.

With one hand on her weapon, she stepped out of the elevator into the garage. Her lips quirked into a smile as she realized they'd brought Gabe's wife's minivan. Joe waved them ahead.

She turned to Ben. "Get in and shut the door. I'll be right behind you."

Julia and Caden went first and Ben followed, the door of the van sliding shut behind him. Maria jumped into the driver's seat as Gabe ran from the stairwell and ducked into the passenger side.

Shots popped from around the corner as they peeled out of the garage.

"You've got to be kidding me," Gabe muttered as Maria pushed the gas pedal to the floor. "My wife is going to kill me if I bring the van back with bullet holes in it."

Into his mike, he said, "Chloe, get the locals into the garage. Tell them their perp was firing at us as we were leaving." He paused. "Yeah, I know they're gonna have questions. They can ask them in Sea Breeze."

The van bounced out the exit door, its big engine roaring as Maria pushed it to its limits. A diaper rolled out from under the seat. Maria kicked it back with her foot. "Uh, Gabe?"

He looked down, grinned. "My wife's car. I thought I explained that. Hey, one of these days, you'll have a couple of kids and a minivan and you'll be trying to figure out how to change a diaper at a state park."

A siren whooped as Joe Sheehan passed them and pulled into the lane in front of them, lights flashing.

Maria looked up at the rearview mirror. The

nanny looked white and Ben didn't look much better. "You guys okay back there?"

Ben answered as he leaned forward to turn on the video player for Caden. "We're fine. What's going to happen when we get home?"

Gabe answered, "It's pretty obvious that someone is trying to get to you. I'd like to put you in a safe house."

Gabe's phone rang. "Sloan," he answered.

Maria kept her eyes on the road and Joe's flashing lights up ahead. Deep breath. They weren't clear yet.

"Mm-hmm. Okay. I'll let them know. You follow up and we'll meet back in Sea Breeze." He hung up the phone and turned to Maria. "You know those names you gave Chloe to check out? Local police just picked one of them up trying to ditch a gun in a holding pond. They think he's our shooter."

Ben leaned forward again. "So it's over?"

Gabe shrugged. "They caught the guy with a gun."

"They'll try to match the ballistics with the evidence they're collecting at the hotel. If it's a match then, yes, it's over." And so was Maria's job as Ben's bodyguard. He wouldn't need her anymore. Being caught up in the moment last night was one thing. A person like Ben wanting her around after what had happened today, that was another thing altogether.

She felt like she was on a tightrope, swaying. Any moment there would be free fall.

"I think you should be cautious until the lab reports are complete." She didn't look at him, but caught his glance in the rearview mirror.

"I just had the alarm system upgraded." He looked from Maria to Gabe. "We'll stay inside, change the codes, keep the alarm on, whatever it takes."

When Gabe nodded, Ben's shoulders relaxed. His eyes met hers in the mirror. "There's the ball tomorrow night. I have to do a broadcast from there. My last regular broadcast for Weather 24."

She looked back at the road. The last thing she wanted at this point was to spend a romantic night—on camera, no less—with Ben.

Chicken? Yes.

How had she gotten to this point?

Right—men. The one sitting beside her who had started this whole thing. His cohorts at the police department. The one in the backseat with soft gray eyes that she couldn't seem to say no to…and the little one sleeping in the car seat. How in the world was she expected to fight against all that male persuasiveness?

She pulled into Ben's driveway.

He unbuckled Caden from the car seat and lifted him into his arms. "Do you mind walking us in?"

Maria walked to the door with the boys—Julia was more than ready to get home and went straight to her own car.

Ben's home had an old-fashioned look, with its large windows and hand-scraped, wide-planked wood floor. The furniture was comfortable, not fancy. He laid Caden on the couch and smoothed a soft blanket over him before turning to Maria. "I'm sorry, Maria."

"For what? I knew pretty much from the beginning what I was getting into." She walked to the mantel. He had pictures set up in colorful frames. A laughing Ben had his arm around a blonde with a full, pregnant belly. "Your wife?"

"The child psychologists think it's important for Caden to have reminders of her around." His eyes seemed to apologize.

He slid a hand across the small of her back and she eased away from him, setting the picture back on the mantel. "Ben, despite everything, I'm thankful I got to know you. Glad we were able to put the past behind us and become a sort of friends."

He took a step closer, crowding her. "I thought

we established last night that what we feel for each other is not friendship. Maria, I've never had anyone on my side—not the way you are."

Her heart tumbled and landed somewhere in the vicinity of her feet. Maria, who wasn't scared of anything, was terrified by what she was starting to feel for this man.

In her job, she walked through crime scenes every day. Blood, death—you name it, she could deal with it. But if anything happened to Ben, it would tear her to shreds. "Listen, I think you're mistaking gratitude for something more than what it is. I helped you out of a tight spot. That's all."

He dropped his hand. "Okay, then. I think you're wrong, but I can't tell you what you're feeling."

His eyes were dark with hurt when the last thing she wanted to do was cause him more pain. But she wasn't a part of this family. It wasn't for her to choose. "Be careful, okay? Even though the guy's in custody, we still need to go through everything carefully and make sure all the loose ends match up."

He nodded and she left, closing the door behind her with a quiet click. She waited for the beep of the alarm as he armed it, then ran for Gabe's van, throwing herself inside and bursting into tears.

"Maria?" The anxiety in Gabe's voice would've

been amusing if she'd been able to catch her breath.

"Just drive, Gabe."

He did, while she completely lost her cool. Ten shuddering, sniveling minutes later, the tears began to slow. Her breath came in hitching gasps, like a baby who'd cried too long.

Gabe cleared his throat. "What—"

"Don't." She wiped her nose on a baby wipe she found in the glove compartment. "Just...don't."

A couple of rogue tears dripped off her jaw.

That did it. She was going to have to do something drastic to get even with the cops who set her up on this date. It wasn't enough just to play a practical joke.

A new sob choked out despite her best effort to hold it in. Because she knew for a fact now.

She was in love with everyone's favorite weatherman, Ben Storm.

Maria stared into the mirror, barely recognizing the woman she saw there. She was used to seeing herself with wild, springy curls and a dangerous look in her eyes. Instead, she saw a woman with hair that would now behave and sad eyes. She'd keep the hair.

But those sad eyes had to go.

Chloe knocked on the bathroom door. "You ready for me?"

"Could I ever be ready for you?" Four-inch heels were Chloe's regular M.O. Maria wore four-inch heels only under duress, but she'd be willing to bet that the box on her bed held a pair at least that high.

Chloe had an overnight bag stuffed to the gills with girly stuff. She pulled the towel off Maria's hair and sighed. "Girl, we've got some work to do."

With the dryer blowing her hair into submission, Maria stared at the dress she would wear tonight.

The gown was a simple white organza column with gathers that fell from the bodice to the floor and one tiny row of rhinestones at the top. She felt like a princess wearing it—and she felt like an impostor. She wasn't made to do this. She was meant for barking orders at crime scenes and drinking cop-shop coffee and trading war stories at the precinct.

This…whatever it was with Ben was an illusion. It had started out that way and it would end that way. It was a joke, a publicity stunt. It *wasn't* real.

And drat it all if her eyes didn't fill again at that

thought. She'd been certain after the embarrassing scene with Gabe that she was completely cried out. She blinked back the tears, hoping Chloe hadn't seen them.

The blow dryer clicked off. Chloe's dark brown eyes narrowed in question, her red hair fuzzing a little in the humid bathroom. "Maria?"

Maria shook her head, not daring to trust her voice.

Chloe dropped onto the stool beside her. "It's Ben, isn't it?"

Maria sniffed. "How'd you know?"

"There's a look we get on our face that's totally recognizable to someone who's been there before. And oh, honey, have I been there." Her friend's eyes filled with sympathetic tears.

Maria reached for a roll of toilet paper. "I was so mad at those guys for making me do this—and then before I knew it, I was charmed. It was all a setup, but I fell for him anyway."

"People aren't like science, Maria. There is no cut-and-dried right answer." Chloe picked up a comb and hairspray and stood, working Maria's hair into long, looping curls with a curling iron as she talked. "I know this must seem crazy to you. You're straight-up, Maria, like this giant beacon for the rest of us to follow—you always know where you're going."

Her hair in the mirror looked more like wet poodle than red carpet. Some beacon. She made a face.

"I'm serious. We all admire you because you're *so* single-minded, so determined. And that's a great quality to have—on a case. But sometimes, when you get to the fork in the road and you have to choose between adventure and logic, it's okay to choose adventure."

"I don't know what you're talking about." Maria squirted some cream into her hands and rubbed it in gentle patting motions onto her face, the way the lady at the salon had showed her. Logic was important.

Chloe pulled her hair. "Oops, sorry. Accident."

Yeah, right.

Once again, Chloe dropped Maria's hair and sat down beside her. This time, her voice was quiet. "If you trust in God—and I know you do—your life is in His hands. He'll be beside you every step of the way, no matter what path you choose."

Chloe stood and rolled another piece of Maria's hair onto the curling iron. "Personally, I think the guys were right."

Maria glared at her in the mirror.

"Not to set you up, I don't mean that. But seriously, you need a life outside the police department. Maria, you don't even have a Christmas tree."

"I do, too." Maria tried to turn her head, but Chloe jerked it back into place. "It's in the kitchen."

"That sad-looking crocheted thing? It looks like your grandmother's pot holder."

Maria tried not to smile, but couldn't help it. "It *was* my grandmother's pot holder. The Christmas one."

"Hold still. I need to get these pins in the right… spot—there. What do you think?"

Her hair was light brown and shot with golden streaks. Blown out and tamed, it curled halfway down her back. "Wow. I think you're a genius."

"I know I am. I'll see you on the purple carpet?" Chloe laughed.

Gabe's wife, Sailor, had gone with purple instead of the traditional red since they were raising money for a local children's charity whose colors were purple and white. "Of course. I wouldn't back out on this now."

Chloe picked up her bag of girl stuff and walked through Maria's apartment toward the front door. "Oh, I can't believe I almost forgot."

She pulled a file folder from the bag. "I kept working on those names you gave me to track down. I finally got a definitive answer on them. The guy Ben beat out for his present job is on assignment in North Africa. I talked directly with his cameraman. He's actually there."

"And the assistant he fired? The one that got arrested?" Maria flipped through the file, but looked up at Chloe.

"Had an alibi for the day the chocolates were set up. He was at an out-of-state luncheon with about forty of his closest friends. I talked to three of them. They said there was no way he could've left and come back because his girlfriend would've missed him." She shrugged. "It's not airtight, but it also leaves room for someone else to be involved."

Maria blew out a breath. "I was afraid of that."

"Wanna share?" Chloe had her hand on the doorknob.

Maria tossed the file on the coffee table. "It's just a feeling really, but Ben said something about his brother-in-law trying to get custody of Caden. It sounded off to me."

Chloe nodded. "I'll try to run down a picture and pass it out to the guys who will be on duty tonight. Maria, please be careful. This whole situation is downright weird." She walked out the door, but instead of closing it, stuck her head back in. "Oh, and Maria—wear the high heels."

SEVEN

Ben's stomach was in knots as he pulled up at an old house on the waterfront where Maria rented a garage apartment. He'd left Caden at home with Julia, with the alarm on and instructions not to open the door to anyone.

At Maria's door, Ben paused. He had so many conflicting emotions. He respected her feelings, her fear that his emotions were based on gratitude and not love, but how could he not love this fiercely smart, protective scientist? She got to him in a way that no one ever had.

Silently, he placed his hand on the door. *Lord, I pray for Your will. Your guidance. Your hand over us tonight.*

The door opened and Maria stood in the opening, light gilding her hair. He swallowed hard. "You look absolutely beautiful."

A sweet smile curved her lips. "I'd have to say you clean up pretty well, too."

He shook his head. "No, really, there's no comparison."

"Ready?" She picked up a black-velvet wrap and evening bag from the end of her brown-leather sofa.

"I asked the camera crew to meet us at the ball rather than film us here," Ben said as she locked the door, "so once we get there, I'll come around the car and help you out. The camera crew will be in front of us, filming for Weather 24. It's all really chaotic, but it'll be over fast." He held her hand as she took the last of the steps, stealing another look at her as he held the car door open.

The transformation had been so dramatic. He barely recognized her as the woman with a tangle of wild curls wearing clunky boots and ugly sunglasses—the woman he'd met at the airport the first day. Yet he knew that at heart, this was still the woman with the smart mouth that he loved.

In contrast, the car ride was quiet—too quiet. Ben didn't know what Maria was thinking, but his mind kept replaying that moment at his house. He'd been thinking that she seemed to fit in his home as if she'd always been there, and she'd been thinking that he was mistaking gratitude for love or something like that.

It stung, still.

Being with her was a little bittersweet under the circumstances, but he had to see this through. He pulled up at the hotel where the Christmas ball was being held. He looked at Maria. "Showtime."

"Ben, wait. There's something you need to know."

His heart started an unsteady beat. Had she changed her mind about him?

"We're not sure that the man they arrested in Destin is the one who's been targeting you." In the shadows of the car, her eyes were dark with worry. "Just be aware, okay?"

His throat tight, he nodded and pushed open the door of the car. They stepped out into madness. People shouting, cameras flashing. Ben curved his arm around Maria's waist and smiled. And wondered—who in this crowd wanted to kill him?

Tension strung tight inside him, a taut wire ready to snap. Where did he find peace when everything inside him just wanted this to be over?

Was it too much to ask that he be allowed to be a dad to his son? This kind of glitz, as fun as it could be, wasn't his gig. It wasn't any kind of reality he wanted.

Maria's spine stiffened under his hand. A few local reporters were shouting questions. One of them pushed through the crowd to get closer to them. Maria pulled him farther along the purple carpet as a uniformed cop stepped up beside the reporters, as well. Another reminder that even in Sea Breeze, he had to be aware.

Maria didn't have to be reminded. Her eyes were constantly moving on the crowd. He was considering the promo push and sound bite. She was considering his safety.

Her reality was crime scenes and lab tests and he had thrown her into the fire of video cameras, appearances and interviews.

But she'd aced it.

Ben looked down at her and, sensing it, she glanced up at him from under those amazing lashes. He smiled.

Her eyes warmed.

The cameras flashed and amusement flared in her eyes. Perfect.

He waved from the top of the stairs.

And as suddenly as the chaos erupted around them, it ended with their entry into the hotel lobby. Ben took his first deep breath in fifteen minutes and beside him Maria did the same.

"Okay?"

She shook her head as if trying to grasp the reality of what had just happened. "Yeah, I think so. Wow. Do you do that a lot?"

"Only when I absolutely have to, which, thankfully, isn't very often. My speed is more playing in the park with Caden than strolling down the red—I mean, purple—carpet. What about you? What do you do in your spare time?"

"What spare time?"

He laughed, but as they walked through the crowd to the doors of the ballroom, he leaned down toward her ear. "Kids are great for getting your priorities straight. Caden and I are planning to do lots of fishing and boating, hanging out at the beach. Maybe it's time for you to work some spare time into your schedule."

She bit down on her lip, her brown eyes full of more thoughts that she didn't want to or couldn't say as he held the door open for her.

The ballroom at the old hotel on the waterfront sparkled with dozens of Christmas trees. Designers had been commissioned to decorate the trees, which as part of the fundraiser would be auctioned off to the highest bidders.

As Maria and Ben reached the dance floor, the band began a slow, bluesy version of "I'll Be Home for Christmas." Ben turned to Maria and held out an arm toward the dance floor. "Shall we?"

She hesitated, barely noticeable if he hadn't been

looking for it, and stepped into his arms. She fit one hand to his as he closed his other arm around her.

He tried not to imagine holding Maria in his arms for Christmases to come. He tried telling himself he'd only known her for a few days. He tried convincing himself she wasn't a perfect fit for him. It didn't work. His heart had already decided.

He'd like to take his heart and pitch it out the window. Life was complicated enough.

She sighed. He tilted her back so he could see her, and as the music changed, whirled her into a turn. Her eyes widened. Her evening bag flew around and hit him on the leg. "What've you got in there, rocks?"

Then he realized and leaned forward to whisper in her ear. "Please tell me you've got a gun in there."

She lifted her hand to cup the back of his neck and pulled his head forward to whisper in his ear, an unguarded smile spreading across her face. "It's a Glock—nine millimeter."

He laughed, delighted.

A camera flashed.

He whirled her around again, away from the prying eyes of the reporter. He wanted to whisk her away to some private island where they could be alone, away from all the pressures, away from all the outside influences. But ultimately, they had to choose to be together despite all those things.

She had to choose. He had to give her time.

And hopefully time was something he would have plenty of after tonight. No more hopping planes every other day, barely home long enough to get over jet lag before taking off in the air again to another country no one'd ever heard of.

The music changed to a soft, sweet Christmas carol. He pulled her close and tried to breathe. How did this happen? This weekend had started as a final job, but somehow it had turned into the beginning of the rest of his life.

The music drifted. He leaned his head close to hers, letting her unique sweet-and-spicy scent float around him. "Thanks."

"For what?"

He shrugged. "For seeing this through. I know it's a strange thing to be followed around by cameras, and the stalker thing just made it even weirder."

"You know what? I will never, ever admit this to the guys at the precinct, but I'm glad they submitted my name. You and Caden are something special."

As the music wound to a close, the auction was announced. At their table, Gabe was already sitting, a baby girl bouncing on his lap. Ben laughed. "Your date's kind of young, isn't she, Gabe?"

"Yep." The big cop smiled down at his baby. "And I'm gonna be her only date for a long, long time. Things still quiet at your house?"

"Seems so."

On the stage, a beautiful blonde in an emerald-green evening gown took the stage. As she introduced herself as Sailor Sloan, Ben shot a look at Gabe, who shrugged. "Yeah, I know. I totally don't deserve her, but I'm keeping her."

Maria smiled, but didn't say a word. As bidding started on the Christmas trees, Ben watched her carefully.

From pink flamingos and feathers, musical instruments to oversize candies, if it could be imagined, a tree had been decorated with it. But there was one tree that made Maria's eyes light up—the one that looked like an old-fashioned chandelier. Crystal teardrops hung from every branch, like an ice-gilded fantasy.

Most of the trees were going for around five thousand dollars. Ben had promised a donation to the charity and, because he knew what it was like to have a sick child, he would do whatever was within his power to make a difference. He may not have been able to find a cure for childhood diseases, but he could write a check.

"Bids for the tree designed by Crystal Carnival open at three thousand dollars," Sailor Sloan said. "And remember, ladies and gentlemen, each tree is original and unique. The designers have assured me the tree they created will never be reproduced. So, do I hear three thousand for the Crystal Carnival tree?"

A few hands went up.

"How about five? I've got five here to my right. Thank you, John."

"Twenty thousand dollars."

A murmur spread around the room. Sailor didn't blink. "From the back of the room, we have twenty thousand. Do I hear twenty-five?"

Ben glanced around the ballroom with a smile. He'd be happy for the charity to make more money, but he was getting that tree one way or another.

Maria elbowed him. "Way to stay out of the spotlight, Storm."

He shrugged. "I really want that tree. Besides, I promised a donation."

"And *sold* to Mr. Ben Storm. Congratulations." Sailor moved to the next tree.

A young woman arrived at Ben's side with a clipboard. "Your signature, Mr. Storm?"

Ben signed for the tree he'd won and turned to Maria. "I've got to do one last broadcast for Weather 24 and then I'd like to go home, if you don't mind. It's a little silly, but I promised myself that when I was done with this job I would always tuck Caden in at night. Do you mind if we go by there and then I'll take you home?"

"It's not silly to want to tuck your child into bed. And I don't mind at all."

Maria had the car brought around as Ben stationed himself front and center on the purple carpet. There were so many people. Some had gathered by the entrance to watch the broadcast, some were waiting around for their chance to be on national television.

It was impossible to see everyone in the crowd. Maria hoped that the cops stationed outside were keeping a vigilant eye out for anything unusual.

She snugged her wrap over her shoulders, for what little good it did her. Ben had donned an overcoat on top of his tux. He looked amazing, the breeze ruffling his black hair, his gray eyes shining in the television lights. It was no wonder he'd charmed the whole country, with his easy smile and natural charisma. He had the believability factor—important for a weather forecaster—and the smarts to back it up.

Not only that, he was leaving a party where he could easily be the center of attention to go home and tuck his little boy into bed. He was the whole package.

So why did she hesitate? The easy answer was also the right one. It was fear, plain and simple.

She'd always depended on her intelligence, on science, for answers. Even though she was a believer, it wasn't a huge leap of faith for her. There was evidence of God everywhere. Evidence in her own life that God was at work.

Trusting God was easy.

Trusting a man? Not so much.

He could so easily break her heart.

She stepped closer to the cameraman, so she could hear Ben's final remarks. "So I want to say thanks for being with me for the weather every day—for taking this journey with me. I'll be back for special events here at Weather 24, so instead of saying goodbye, I'll just say, see you around. This is Ben Storm for Weather 24. Back to you, Charles."

He held his position, those clear gray eyes so direct on the camera lens, until the cameraman said, "We're clear. Good job, Ben."

Ben shook hands with his cameraman, which led to a back-slapping hug. Then he was walking toward her.

He wrapped his arms around her and lifted her off her feet. The crowd, clapping for Ben already, began to cheer him on.

She slid to her feet, cheeks burning, as Ben opened the car door for her, which she still found to be amusing. None of the men in her life ever remembered that she was female, let alone opened the door for her.

As he drove away, he didn't even look back in the rearview mirror. "I am so glad to be finished with that. I guess there was a time when I loved it, the excitement of being in a new place every few days, but after a while it got to be just another hotel room, just another weather report, you know?"

Maria pulled the wrap around her arms. She'd gone back and watched video clips of him doing the weather, and it was so much more than a weather report. She could totally understand why he was so well-liked. "I don't think the people who watched you saw it that way, Ben. I think they saw a little piece of the world through your eyes that they wouldn't have gotten to see otherwise. And when you visited places that had been damaged,

I never saw sensationalism coming from you, just stories of humanity, if that makes sense."

Ben's throat worked and his voice, when it came, was husky. "I think I'd forgotten why I did the job in the first place. Thanks for reminding me."

"Anytime. So if you don't mind me asking a personal question, it's still going to be important for Caden to have therapy, right?"

"Absolutely. It's one reason I quit. I wanted to be able to be home in the mornings so I can do more of the appointments."

"So will you be able to afford to keep Julia on as your nanny on a local guy's salary?" She didn't know why she was asking, but something he'd said earlier was niggling at the back of her mind.

"Yes. We're really blessed that Caden's grand-parents on his mother's side left him a trust fund. He's basically set for life. The fund will pay Julia's salary and, from here on out, my salary will cover the day-to-day needs." His fingers clenched on the steering wheel. "I always kind of thought that my brother-in-law tried to gain custody of Caden just for the trust fund."

He slammed down on the brake pedal. "Wait. Do you think—"

"Yeah, I do. There's no proof that the assistant tampered with the chocolates. In fact, it would've been really difficult for him to do so, considering he was out of town at the time. Chloe is trying to track down your brother-in-law, but so far she's had no luck."

Ben pulled into his driveway. "Something isn't right. Julia's car should be parked here."

Maria reached under the seat for her purse. "She wouldn't leave Caden. Is it possible they went somewhere?"

"Not likely. Our schedule is pretty regular, even when we're away, like at the condo."

Maria texted Gabe to send backup and that she was going inside with Ben to check things out. When she looked up, Ben's face was white, his phone open in his hand.

"Julia. My brother-in-law Randy made her leave, threatened Caden if she didn't. Maria, Caden's all alone in there with him."

Maria gripped his hand. "Not for long. Let's go."

At the stairs, she took off her high heels. She couldn't move in them and they made way too much noise. "Okay, open the door."

Ben turned the key in the lock and pushed the door open. In the main living area, underneath the Christmas tree, a tall bearded man was seated on the floor with Caden. But what Maria saw was the gun loosely held in his hand.

Ben let out an involuntary breath. The man's head jerked up and he jumped to his feet.

Before Ben could leap forward, Maria put a hand out, stopping him. "We're gonna keep things cool, right, Ben?"

Underneath her palm, she could feel Ben trembling with anger, but his voice was calm. "Maria, meet my brother-in-law, Randy. Randy, this is Maria."

Randy's eyes were red. He'd either stayed awake for days or had been on a bender. But either way, it made him unpredictable. The gun wobbled in his hand.

"Why do you need a weapon, Randy? Do you think you're in danger here?" Maria took a step forward, toward Caden, who hadn't moved, just rocked back and forth on the floor.

"Stop!" Randy pointed the gun at Caden. "Don't make me hurt him."

Ben's voice went low and hard. "You hurt one hair on his head and you won't live to regret it."

"Ben." The last thing they needed to do was freak this guy out more. *Please, God, give me the words to say.*

"Randy, you know you don't want to hurt Caden. He's just a little boy."

His quivering hands turned the gun on her. "You think you're so smart? You don't know me."

Ben's voice cracked through the air. "Randy, that's enough. You can't come in my home and threaten people I love."

Maria's heart stopped only to pick up the beat a tick later twice as fast when Randy pointed the handgun at Ben. "You're in love with her? That's rich. If it's so easy for you to forget my sister, I should've killed her years ago."

The color drained from Ben's face. "You killed Lindsay?"

"It's either get my hands on the trust-fund money or let the drug dealers kill me. I messed up some of their product and, let me tell you, those guys know how to hold a grudge." He laughed, on the edge of hysteria, and the muzzle swung around toward Caden again.

Maria took one step forward.

Randy's face purpled. "Don't do it. Don't come any closer."

Caden rocked on the floor, his favorite car clutched in his hand. He hadn't made eye contact. She prayed that the progress Ben and Julia had made with him hadn't been completely reversed by the trauma of this conflict.

"Randy, think this through. If you hurt Caden, you don't get the money." Maria took another step forward and the gun turned back to her.

She saw his finger move on the trigger. She braced herself for the impact, but Ben lunged in front of her.

He hit the floor, blood blooming on his shirt.

Shock leached the feeling out of her fingers. She moved toward Ben, but Randy shook the gun at her. "Don't."

Tears rolled down Caden's face, but he didn't cry out, just increased the rhythmic rocking, back and forth.

In that second, a red laser dot appeared on Randy's shirt. *Yes*.

Somewhere outside, there was a sniper on her side. She held up a hand, signaling whoever it was to give her a minute more. "Randy, you do realize that you're holding us hostage, don't you? There are police outside who are not going to let you walk away. Your only chance is to put your weapon down and walk out of here with your hands up."

"*What?* The police aren't here. You're lying." He pitched toward the window. Blue-and-red lights flashed on outside.

In that second of inattention, Maria pulled her 9mm from her evening bag and leveled it at Randy. He whirled around, fear on his face. His eyes opened wide when he saw her holding her handgun.

"Put your weapon on the floor," she ordered him. "Do it now."

Ben pushed to his feet beside her, swaying as he stood, his arm dangling, useless. "Randy, listen to Maria, please. Don't make this harder."

The pistol wavered in Randy's hand. He looked at Caden, his face turning red. He lurched toward the boy.

Maria shot. She hit his shoulder and he pitched backward—away from Caden. Randy's gun hit the floor and skimmed away harmlessly.

The door slammed open. Gabe had his weapon drawn, a bulletproof vest over his tux shirt. Cruse Conyers stood behind him, his own tux shirt covered by a vest, as well.

"It's about time y'all got here." Maria had her knee in Randy's back, his arms tucked up behind him.

Ben gathered his little boy in his arms. Caden didn't move, but buried his face in Ben's neck. "It's okay now, bud. You're safe."

A couple of uniformed officers came in behind

Gabe and Cruse to handcuff Randy and haul him out, which they did, as he wailed about police brutality.

Ben left the room with Caden, not even meeting Maria's eyes.

She watched him leave, knowing he was right to walk away from her. If she'd been able to figure out sooner who'd been stalking Ben, she'd have been able to keep Ben from being hurt, to keep his little boy from being traumatized. As it was, she wouldn't be surprised if he never wanted to see her again.

EIGHT

Ben found it hard to sit still in the dark in Caden's room, his mind reeling with the consequences of what had just happened. But right now Caden needed to know that Ben was right here and that he was safe. As the little boy's breathing evened out and his body relaxed, Ben eased out of the room.

Where before there had been chaos, little evidence remained that anything had happened. There was a shadow of a stain on the floor, but all the cops were gone. The lamps were low, the tree lights and the fire lending a soft glow to the room that had seemed so stark and violent a short while ago. Quiet Christmas music played from the surround sound.

Caden's cars were lined up in exact order under the Christmas tree. Ben's eyes pricked. He blinked and blew out a breath. He needed to get hold of himself.

Maria padded out of the kitchen in SBPD sweats that were about four sizes too big for her. She stopped short when she saw him. "I hope it's okay. I didn't want Caden to wake up to reminders of what happened here tonight."

He nodded. "What happened to your dress?"

"Blood spatter evidence." She laughed—a careful laugh, unlike herself. "Strange for someone to be collecting evidence from me when it's usually the other way around."

"Maria—"

"You probably need stitches in that arm, Ben."

"I'm not going to get stitches in my arm—it's fine." He walked toward her. "Maria—"

"Sit down and let me clean it up if you're not going to the hospital. I found your first aid kit in the kitchen." She walked ahead of him to stand by the fireplace.

He followed her and when she pointed at the chair, he grabbed her hands and pulled her close, tucking her head under his chin and holding her. She went rigid.

"I was so scared, Maria. My whole life was in this room, in the hands of a crazy person." His voice cracked.

He felt her take a breath and wrap her fists into

his shirt. And for the first time since they'd gotten home, he relaxed just a little.

"I'm sorry I didn't put it together sooner." Her voice was muffled against his chest, but he didn't want to let go of her, even long enough for a conversation.

"It's my fault. I should've realized when Randy tried to gain custody of Caden that he didn't have Caden's best interest at heart. But I tried to convince myself that he was attempting to hold on to his memory of Lindsay and do the best he could for her son. I was wrong. And I came so close to losing everything." He leaned away so he could see her face. "I just found you. I couldn't take losing you."

She stepped out of his arms and hitched up her pants, making him smile. When she pushed him onto the ottoman and pulled his shirt sleeve off at the seam, he decided he might want to do what she said tonight.

A stream of something cold hit his arm and he yelped. "That *hurt!* Maria, what is that stuff?"

"Antiseptic, Ben. Be a big boy now. It won't be long." She opened a package of butterfly bandages with her teeth and applied them to the four-inch-long gash in his arm, muttering the whole time, something about evidence and bullets being dug out of the wall.

He didn't want to know what she was saying, but got a good idea where her thoughts were leading when she said, "You really should go to the E.R."

"No. If Caden wakes up, I want to be here."

Another paper package lost to her teeth and landed on the floor by her feet. She began wrapping gauze around the wound on his arm. "Hold this."

He held the spot she'd told him as she tore a piece of tape and secured the ends of the gauze. Before she could move away, he grabbed her hands and pulled her down on the ottoman beside him.

When he saw the tears pooled in her eyes, his heart made a painful thump. "What's all this?"

"Ben, you're an amazing guy. And Caden is so precious. It makes me so happy when you say that you care about me." She shrugged. "But I think you both deserve more than an emotionally stunted scientist."

He slid his hands along the sides of her face, and as her eyes drifted closed, tears clinging to the lashes, he brushed his lips over hers. She leaned forward, into the kiss, into him.

Ben eased back, still with his fingers tangled in

her hair, and just looked at her, firelight playing on her face, gold sparks shimmering in her eyes. "You underestimate yourself, Maria."

For a man who hadn't known that he needed her, he craved her presence in his life like the next breath.

A horn honked outside. She jumped away from him, landing on her feet and grabbing at the sweatpants again. He was so in love with her. "My ride. I knew you wouldn't be able to leave Caden."

She reached for the door handle.

"Maria."

She turned her face toward him, light catching on the golden highlights in her hair.

He wanted to go to her, but could see she needed space. "Science is easy, sweetheart. An answer for every question, given enough time to sort it out. People are different—unpredictable. There are no fundamental laws. But you know that feeling when you finally solve a problem?"

She nodded.

"Working things out with someone you love is a thousand times better."

"Harder."

"Worth it." He meant it.

"I—need some time, Ben."

He nodded, his own throat full. She'd saved his

son's life. He owed her so much more than thanks, but it was all he had right now. "Thanks for being here. For choosing to be here when you didn't have to. You saved Caden's life and mine."

She glanced back one more time, nodded. "See you around, Ben."

Ben didn't miss that she'd chosen the words he'd used to say goodbye to his viewing public. The only problem was, he never meant to go back to that job, other than for brief visits. He prayed as he watched her leave. *Please, God, if it's Your will, let her come back to me—for good.*

But she'd said she needed time, so he'd give her time.

He managed five days.

"Back the truck here." He motioned with his hands toward the driveway leading to her garage apartment. "Easy."

In front of him, Caden mimicked, "Easy."

Ben laughed out loud. "Okay, bud, you ready to go get her? It's all or nothing now."

Caden nodded. "Go get 'er. Get Maria."

Ben rang the doorbell at Maria's apartment as the truck backed into her driveway with a piercing beep. Sigh. No such thing as a surprise with something this big. But maybe...

She opened the door, her curly hair tucked up

into a knot with a pencil stuck through it, little pieces springing free to bounce around her face.

Suddenly tongue-tied, Ben stared. She looked as beautiful—*more* beautiful—in her jeans and T-shirt with her hair all scrunchy than she did in her glamorous clothes at the resort. He was so toast. Caden said, "We brought you a present. It's pretty."

Her eyes darted to Ben's. He shrugged and tilted his head toward the driveway down below, where the Christmas tree was being carefully taken down from the flatbed truck. "I couldn't help but notice you didn't have one."

A smile started in the corners of her mouth. "That's not strictly true, but I've been told that I could use an upgrade."

He called down, "Bring her on up, boys."

"It's too much, Ben."

"But you like it?" Did his insecurity show in his voice? Because he could feel his every emotion hanging by a thread here.

The guys manhandled the tree into position in Maria's small sitting room. It touched the ceiling, but he thought it went with her eclectic mix of antiques and flea market finds.

"Wow." She circled the tree, touching the precious crystals. "It's gorgeous."

"There's a special one, Maria, a really special one. Right, Dad?" Caden danced on his toes by the tree.

Ben picked Caden up. "That's right, Caden. There's a special ornament for Maria."

Maria saw it then. Tucked amid all the glitter and shine, was one very glittery, very shiny ornament—a circle of platinum tied with a black ribbon to a branch. "Oh."

Ben slid the ring off the branch and said, "I know this has been an unorthodox courtship, but Capo and I have talked about it. We would really like it if you would do us the honor of joining our family."

He dropped to one knee and beside him Caden did the same. Maria's throat threatened to close up on her. Ben held the diamond ring in his palm and said, "Maria Fuentes, I love you. Please, marry me?"

She shook her head, her heart pounding. She wanted the dream life that he was holding out to her, wanted it more than she'd ever imagined she could. But— "We can't get married, Ben. You don't even know me."

"I know the important stuff."

She paced away from him, saw her badge sitting on the kitchen counter and spun around. "My job takes me away from home at weird hours of the day and night. Sometimes I get consumed by it."

"We have a nanny. And part of what I love about you is that you are willing to work for justice. You're strong and independent. Tough."

She didn't feel tough. She felt like butter melting into a mushy puddle. The diamond glimmered in the ring Ben held. "All I know how to be is a scientist and a cop. I don't know anything about being a mom or a wife."

"Don't you love us?" Caden blurted.

"Oh, baby." The tears started. "Of course I love you."

Ben's deep voice was rough with emotion as he stood to look in her eyes. She didn't have any doubt that she could see his heart in his eyes. "What about Caden's dad? Do you love him, too?"

She bit her lip. And taking a deep breath, nodded. "I do, Ben, so much."

Ben pulled Caden to his feet and handed him his backpack full of cars, sending him to the kitchen table to play. In seconds, he had her in his arms, her face pressed against his chest, right against his heart.

"Sweetheart, there's no scientific formula for marriage, but I have a hypothesis I'd like to try out."

She tilted her face to look at him, gave a shaky grin. "What's that?"

"Love plus marriage equals a happy, chaotic life, filled with joy and laughter, a few tears and lots of good memories."

Maria drew her brows together as if deep in thought. "It's an interesting theory. I think it will take years of testing to come to a plausible conclusion. Do you think you're up for that, Mr. Storm?"

Ben slid the ring onto Maria's finger and, pulling her close against his chest, dropped his forehead close to hers. "I do."

EPILOGUE

Maria dug her toes in a little deeper, letting the silky sand slide over her feet. The Gulf of Mexico was almost smooth today, a rare green-flag day. She drifted close to sleep, listening to Caden's squeals of laughter as Ben chased him through the slow rolling surf.

They'd come back to stay at the Emerald Island resort, renting a plain old condo this time. Their stay in the penthouse seemed like a long-ago dream, though in reality it had only been a few months.

A whirlwind Christmas courtship had turned into a New Year's wedding for friends and family. And for someone who had been so unsure of herself in this arena, Maria found herself newly enchanted every day with her husband and son.

Cold water dripped onto her sun-warmed stomach. She squealed and ripped off her sunglasses, pointing at Ben, who held a dripping Caden over her. "Oh—you are in so much trouble. I promise, I *will* get you back."

"Like you promised you'd get even with the guys at the precinct for setting you up on the date weekend with me?" He dropped onto the towel beside her while Caden dug his dump truck into the sand.

She chuckled. "It's almost better not to do anything. They're scared every time they open their lockers. And forget coming into my lab." She stretched in satisfaction. "It's much quieter in there these days."

Ben spread his fingers across her stomach. "How's peanut?"

"Hungry, as usual. I'm not even showing yet and I'm eating twice my body weight. This should be fun." She looked over to see Caden carefully constructing something out of sand. "Hey, Capo, whatcha working on?"

Their five-year-old didn't even look up. "It's a fingerprint fuming chamber."

Ben raised one eyebrow at Maria.

"Hey, you're the one who told me to show him the lab."

Caden plowed over the square he'd just built. "Oh no, it just got hit by a tornado. It was an EF-5, Dad."

Maria struggled not to smile as Ben choked out his response. "Impressive."

A little while later, as they packed up their things and headed back to the condo, Ben put his arm around Maria. "I think, from all evidence, you definitely believe in love. What do you think? Come up with any conclusions about that hypothesis yet?"

She snorted. "*Pshh*—love. It's chemistry. Pheromones and dopamine. PEA. Adrenaline." She glanced at him under her lashes to see his reaction. His mouth dropped open.

Then he smiled and said, "Yep. And then there's the HEA."

She made a face. "What are you talking about?"

He pulled her close for a kiss. Her knees went weak. That silly chemistry.

Ben whispered in her ear. "And they lived Happily Ever After."

* * * * *

Dear Reader,

From the first day Maria walked onto a crime scene, I knew she was a character to be reckoned with. She would need a very special hero because Maria didn't really believe in love—at least not for her.

It took some meddlesome coworkers and the love of a very special child to bring Ben and Maria together under the Christmas tree.

I pray that your Christmas season is blessed with love and laughter. And that, like Maria, you have found that God's love isn't really scientific or rational, but that it's His gift to you, all the same.

Please visit my Web site at: www.stephanienewtonbooks.com for more information, or e-mail me at newtonwriter@gmail.com. I love hearing from readers!

Merry Christmas,

Stephanie Newton

QUESTIONS FOR DISCUSSION

1. Maria thinks she's got life figured out, but a surprise by her coworkers sends her reeling. Describe a time when you were surprised by life and had to scramble to figure out your next step.

2. How do you handle life's surprises—the good ones or bad ones?

3. Maria blamed Ben for her losing the scholarship that would've sent her to college. How does she later take responsibility?

4. Ben had to make a difficult choice, but chose to put his child in front of his career. How did his faith make it easier to make that choice?

5. Maria sees Ben's tattered Bible and thinks that he must be all right. What do you think? Is a man's dedication to studying the Bible an indicator of what kind of man he is?

6. Ben learns that he can open his heart to love. What does Maria learn at the end of the book that makes it possible for her to have a future with Ben?

LARGER-PRINT BOOKS!

GET 2 FREE LARGER-PRINT NOVELS PLUS 2 FREE MYSTERY GIFTS

Love Inspired®

SUSPENSE
RIVETING INSPIRATIONAL ROMANCE

Larger-print novels are now available...

YES! Please send me 2 FREE LARGER-PRINT Love Inspired® Suspense novels and my 2 FREE mystery gifts (gifts are worth about $10). After receiving them, if I don't wish to receive any more books, I can return the shipping statement marked "cancel". If I don't cancel, I will receive 4 brand-new novels every month and be billed just $4.74 per book in the U.S. or $5.24 per book in Canada. That's a saving of over 20% off the cover price. It's quite a bargain! Shipping and handling is just 50¢ per book.* I understand that accepting the 2 free books and gifts places me under no obligation to buy anything. I can always return a shipment and cancel at any time. Even if I never buy another book, the two free books and gifts are mine to keep forever.

110 IDN E5TF   310 IDN E5TR

Name _____ (PLEASE PRINT)

Address _____ Apt. #

City _____ State/Prov. _____ Zip/Postal Code

Signature (if under 18, a parent or guardian must sign)

Mail to Steeple Hill Reader Service:
IN U.S.A.: P.O. Box 1867, Buffalo, NY 14240-1867
IN CANADA: P.O. Box 609, Fort Erie, Ontario L2A 5X3
Not valid for current subscribers to Love Inspired Suspense larger-print books.

Are you a current subscriber to Love Inspired Suspense books and want to receive the larger-print edition?
Call 1-800-873-8635 or visit www.morefreebooks.com.

* Terms and prices subject to change without notice. Prices do not include applicable taxes. Sales tax applicable in N.Y. Canadian residents will be charged applicable provincial taxes and GST. Offer not valid in Quebec. This offer is limited to one order per household. All orders subject to approval. Credit or debit balances in a customer's account(s) may be offset by any other outstanding balance owed by or to the customer. Please allow 4 to 6 weeks for delivery. Offer available while quantities last.

Your Privacy: Steeple Hill Books is committed to protecting your privacy. Our Privacy Policy is available online at www.SteepleHill.com or upon request from the Reader Service. From time to time we make our lists of customers available to reputable third parties who may have a product or service of interest to you. If you would prefer we not share your name and address, please check here. ☐

Help us get it right—We strive for accurate, respectful and relevant communications. To clarify or modify your communication preferences, visit us at www.ReaderService.com/consumerschoice.

TYLISLP10